Dennis Milam Bensie

ROBINSON, IL

and other flash fiction stories

Cover and interior design by Catherine Treadgold

Contact: sampson_cutter@yahoo.com

ISBN: 978-1-7362822-1-2 (print)

This book is dedicated to my dear friend, R2

Acknowledgments

SPECIAL THANKS TO BALLARD WRITER'S CRITIQUE Group and Seattle Writer's Group-Daylight Hours.

Thank you to Jim, Eric, JR, Matt, and Catherine.

What is Flash Fiction?

FLASH FICTION IS A GENRE OF fiction, defined as a very short story. While there is no set word count that separates flash fiction from more traditional short stories, flash fiction can be as short as a few words, while short stories typically run for several pages.

Contents

Denny

FOUR-YEAR-OLD DENNY DOESN'T HAVE A CARE in the world. A modest front yard is his kingdom; a nearby, urban creek is his moat. His stay-at-home mother has set her iron and ironing board up just inside the front door of his castle. She pensively does her ironing while keeping a close eye on her precious son.

The boy has a charmed life. He's the prince of Clay Street. He loves to ride his red tricycle up and down the sidewalk in front of his house while Mom watches him like a hawk. Denny rides the twelve-foot stretch from the front-porch steps to the end of the sidewalk, then turns the trike around and rides it right back towards the house.

Back and forth, back and forth for hours, just like a pendulum.

The child turns his trike around for the umpteenth time today and sees a small garter snake on the sidewalk. It's the first time he's ever seen a live snake, and the sight of it slithering around jolts him. He's overwhelmed and lets out a high-pitched scream.

He screams and screams and screams.

Out of the blue, Denny's mother charges onto the scene with a garden hoe. With insane determination, she starts maniacally hacking at the snake. The woman has an unusually strong swing for being in her mid-forties. She slams the blade of the hoe down on the sidewalk with loud clang, over and over. With each swing of the hoe, the tiny serpent is sliced to bits.

It's a gory battle. For an instant, Denny doesn't recognize his own mother. She's turned into a violent killing machine. Her eyes are crazed, and her face is all twisted up. She maniacally slashes away at the snake for five solid minutes, cutting it into twenty jagged pieces. The frantic woman makes deep grunting noises as she kicks all the pieces into the grass out of her boy's sight. She's gone above and beyond the call of duty to eliminate his problem. The creature didn't stand a chance.

Denny's mom throws the hoe to the side and dramatically swoops her son up into her arms like a rag doll. The devoted mother coddles her child, checking every inch of him to make sure he isn't hurt. Mom sobs and hugs her boy so tight that he can barely breathe. The snake is deader than dead, and Denny deeply understands that his mommy will always protect him.

What Denny can't possibly know yet is that he's a miracle child. The prince of Clay Street is his mother's only heir: an irreplaceable legacy.

She had seven miscarriages before she was able to carry a baby full term.

The Kiddie Pool

It's six o'clock in the morning, the first day of summer vacation, and I'm very excited.

Mom carries me into my grandma's house. Grandma and Grandpa are going to babysit me and my twin cousins, Delia and Donna, so our moms can go to work at the factory across town.

Mom gently lays me on Grandma's couch and kisses me goodbye. Before I go back to sleep, I hear Mom remind Grandma, "Don't let him get wet at the kiddie pool. I don't want him to get another sore throat."

Me and the twins will all be in first grade this fall. I don't have any brothers or sisters, so I've really been looking forward to spending the whole summer with the girls at my grandma's house.

Grandpa leaves after lunch and Grandma announces that we are all going swimming. I want to go and splash around and get wet with the twins real bad, but I know I'm not supposed to. I don't say anything and hope that Grandma forgets what my mom said to her this morning.

Delia and Donna go to bathroom together to put on their brand-new swimsuits, but I don't have one. This is my mom's way of making sure I don't get wet. My swim trunks are hidden at home.

Grandma comes out of her bedroom with something in her hand.

"Do you want to play with the girls at the kiddie pool?" she asks me.

I nod my head, "Yes."

"Then you can wear this. It should fit you just fine. You can get a little bit wet and I won't tell your mother."

Grandma hands me a one-piece *girls' swimsuit*. It's pink and has flowers and a skirt attached. I don't know what to say.

"It's one of the twins' old swimsuits. It's been here since last summer."

Grandma looks real happy for me, but I'm confused. I don't know if I should put the pink swimsuit on or not. It's for a little girl and it feels way too naughty for me to wear anyone's clothes but my own.

"You want to go swimming, don't you?" Grandma says.

I shake my head "no" and give the swimsuit back.

We pack up the station wagon and head to the park. My twin cousins run to the entrance waving their arms and singing, while Grandma and I find a bench close by. I'm very sad and I can tell that my grandma is sad, too. We sit and watch the other kids play and have fun. After a while she takes my hand.

"Follow me, kiddo."

She walks me to the car, opens the back door and hands me the pink swimsuit with flowers again. I can't believe she brought it to the pool with her. She bends over and gets right in my face.

"I know you want to put this on. Go ahead. Nobody can see you."

I tilt my head down to the ground. My grandma wants me to go swimming more than I do. I'm scared. My eyes are starting to water like I'm going to cry.

"You're going to put this swimsuit on and go have fun with the girls. Understand me?"

She's getting mad at me. She makes a mean face and starts jerking all my clothes off, even my underwear. I don't like being naked in front of anyone. She pulls the pink swimsuit up over my waist and spins me around and ties the ties in a bow at the back of my neck. She's right: the suit fits. I'm afraid to say anything.

"Now run along and get in the water," she grunts.

My stomach hurts as I go over to the kiddie pool and step into the knee-deep water with the twins. I wish the water was deeper so I could hide all the way up to my neck. I've never been this uncomfortable in my whole life.

Delia and Donna look at me, confused. I think they can tell that I'm upset, but they're afraid to say anything.

There are lots of kids in the pool today, but I don't see any of my friends. The big kids are all in the big-kid pool. But there are moms and dads all over the place. I keep wondering why nobody says anything about a boy wearing a girl's swimsuit in the pool.

I see my grandma sitting on the bench on the other side of the parking lot. She's smiling and laughing with a man I don't recognize. They're smoking cigarettes. I've never seen Grandma smoke a cigarette before.

Today's the worst day of my life. My throat's getting sore all over again.

Donna pulls me aside and whispers in my ear, "It's okay. You just look like a girl with really short hair."

People really think I'm a girl. Maybe I'm supposed to be a girl. I don't want to be a girl.

My grandma's one of those bad women.

The man kisses her on the mouth and it makes me snap.

I pull the pink swimsuit down to my knees and pee in the water right in front of a lifeguard. All the little girls around me scream and a loud whistle is blown. Everyone's told to get out of the water and the kiddie pool is quickly closed down.

Grandma leaves the man at the bench and stomps over to get us. I don't even get to dry off before she jerks me into the back of the station wagon.

No one talks to me the rest of the day. Nobody dares mention the kiddie pool when Mom picks me up at four in the afternoon.

We don't go back the park the rest of the summer.

Have a Cookie

My first graders bring in something they like from the outside world to share for *Show and Tell* every Tuesday morning.

Martin Taccone does his presentation last. He slowly walks up to the head of the class carrying a heavy satchel that looks like it has a bowling ball in it. He carefully takes out something wrapped in a blanket. It's a ceramic figure that looks like Mammy, the large black woman who takes care of Scarlett O'Hara in *Gone With the Wind.*

I can't breathe.

Martin and his family are white. Why on earth do they have a black statue like that in a small town like Robinson, Illinois?

Where do you even get such a thing these days?

Martin pulls the top off and shows us that the Mammy is actually a cookie jar.

"This is from my kitchen," he explains to the class. "My mom bakes cookies and puts them in here for me and my brothers to eat. We call her the 'The Cookie Mammy.'"

The skin tone of Mammy is pure black: nothing brown or lifelike about it. The whites of her oversized eyes bug out like a cartoon character and she has big, red, pursed lips. She's wearing a red and white checkered dress and a kerchief on her head. And, of course, she's got a white apron over her big skirt.

I'm a bit scared to look at Martin holding the Mammy cookie jar right in front of my class. My knees are knocking.

In all my years of teaching, this is the most shocking *Show and Tell* item I have ever seen. It's nothing but a sad reminder of slavery in America.

The Taccone boy is a wonderful and expressive student. Thankfully, he talks mostly about the different kinds of cookies his mom makes for his family.

But I'm still uncomfortable looking at that garish cookie jar. I pray to God that none of the students use the "N-word" today.

My school district teaches the Civil War right out of a history textbook in the higher grades. But a Mammy cookie jar is the type of image America should just forget. It's sinister and not nice.

I hope to God that that cookie jar is an antique. What if Martin's mom got it new at Walmart? That would make no sense because there are almost no black people in Robinson.

We have a few Asians and Jews and Hispanics, but no one really thinks about them being different. They don't act different and we don't talk about their color. They just blend in with the rest of us. This isn't a big city like Chicago—we all get along.

Martin Taccone finishes his presentation and takes the lid

off of the Mammy and hands out homemade chocolate chip cookie to each of his classmates.

I can finally breathe a sigh of relief.

While the kids are all at recess, a conversation with the principal is in order. He gives me the go-ahead to call Martin's mother. But all Mrs. Taccone wants to do is have a political debate. I explained to her that the principal and I feel that it was inappropriate for Martin to bring the Mammy cookie jar in for *Show and Tell.* Something less controversial would be safer for first grade. I remind her that school isn't *Gone With the Wind.*

She defends the cookie jar, claiming that it's a family heirloom. She dug it out of storage after that big, national news story happened where the white guy shot and killed that young black kid.

Believe me, I understand the need for teachable moments, but a cookie jar in our small town has nothing to do with him getting shot—and not all parents are going to agree with the way she raises her three sons.

"The classroom—*my* classroom—must remain neutral. We don't need to get into such complicated matters in first grade. There will be plenty of time for that when the children are older," I tell her.

Mrs. Taccone and I go back and forth at each other for almost half an hour and we finally agree to disagree about when and how to teach civil rights. She promises me that she will pay better attention to what her son brings to school for *Show and Tell* in the future.

It's Tuesday again. I assume it's going to be just another typical morning of *Show and Tell.* Again, the last student to do his presentation before lunch is Martin Taccone. I see him dragging that same bowling ball bag to the head of the class.

I'm dumbfounded as he reaches into the bag and pulls out that same cookie jar, only this time Mammy has been painted solid black: the skin, the eyes and lips, the clothes are all the same color of black.

Not a skin tone of black: black like coal.

All of Mammy's details are gone.

If I hadn't seen the cookie jar before, I might not have known what it was at first.

Yet across the midsection is hand printed, BLACK LIVES MATTER in red paint.

"The news makes me sad," Martin tells the class. "Ferguson, Missouri is only one hundred seventy-five miles away from Robinson, Illinois."

Martin's mother obviously figured out the distance for him and coached him on what to say for my *Show and Tell*.

"My mom and I painted this jar black when he died. We baked cookies in memory of Michael Brown."

Martin Taccone hands out homemade cookies to the class once again; this time they are white chocolate chip with nuts.

I'm allergic to nuts.

Cornstalks

My husband and I bought a house out in the country on an acre of land. We spent as much time as we could outdoors. He took a lot of pride in caring for the yard, while I loved to spend time in my vegetable garden. We set up a fancy swing for our son Wayne to encourage him to get out of the house more often.

We thought that living in the country was safer than the city until some corn started turning up missing from my garden. Whole stalks were being ripped out of the dirt every day. The stalks and the ears were nowhere to be found. It looked deliberate, but the corn wasn't even ready yet.

Our neighbors were all nice people; families just like us. Henry and I caught Susan at her mailbox one morning and told her about my missing corn.

"I just don't understand why anyone would come on our property and rip up my corn like that … stalk and all. I'd just give them the corn if they'd come to the door and ask."

"You know, people are crazy. Remember last year … someone got into the Bates house up the road. All they took was a bag of clothes that had been set aside to donate uptown at the clothing center," Susan said.

My husband piped up, "Whoever's stealing our corn must need it more than we do. We'd better start locking our doors just in case."

Later that evening, I went to the backyard to call my boy in for supper. Wayne was playing on his swing set and didn't see me.

He had a cornstalk in his hand.

He'd broken the stalk down to about two feet of stem and just one long leaf at the top. He was talking to the stalk in a funny voice … but it was more like he was pretending to be the stalk.

I watched as he walked around holding the stalk up about head high like a flag: the long leaf was hanging down his forearm. He was having a good time flipping the leaf around. I could tell that he loved the leaf blowing back and forth in the wind.

The mystery had been solved, but I wasn't sure what to think about my son stealing.

"Wayne, Honey, it's time for supper," I announced, pretending I didn't see his odd toy.

Wayne dropped the cornstalk in a panic. He looked real embarrassed. I waited until bedtime after his dad was asleep to question him about stealing from my garden.

"Son, why are you taking cornstalks from the garden?" I asked. Wayne got upset and started to cry. His reaction surprised me.

"It's okay, Son. I just want to know what's going on. You

had your dad and me scared that a stranger was stealing from us."

My son was so disturbed that he couldn't answer my question.

"Listen, Son … please don't pull any more of my garden up. Understand?"

"Yes. I'm so sorry, Mom."

He paused and asked, "Do you still love me?"

I was stunned that he would ask such a question.

"Of course I do," I answered. "I'll always love you, Wayne, no matter what."

My husband loves Wayne, too, but they don't have much in common. I see other dads with their sons tagging along: men going fishing or watching their sports. I wish my guys did stuff together like that, but they just don't have that kind of relationship.

I said to my husband more than once, "Henry, why don't you take Wayne outside and toss the ball around with him or something? Go have some fun." He always ignored me.

I try my best to stay out of my son's business. But I started paying more attention to what my son was playing with after we talked about the cornstalks. I noticed him making a bunch of toys in his bedroom. He was always putting string or yarn or long strips of paper on some sort of a stick. Wayne is a creative boy but he's always hidden his creations.

I got a big surprise changing Wayne's bed sheets one morning. I found a new Barbie doll hidden in the box springs. All of a sudden, it made sense to me: the cornstalks were his dolls. The leaves were his doll's hair. I put the doll back where I found it.

I knew my husband wouldn't allow his son to have a doll.

He never handled his emotions well. I love Henry, but I wish he were a better dad.

I guess Wayne must "need" a doll. He probably saved his lunch money to buy it. The boy's obviously clever enough to make substitute dolls out of whatever he could find before he got that Barbie. The thought of him going hungry so he could get a Barbie doll made me sad. His playing with dolls wasn't hurting anybody.

There're all kinds of messages hidden with that Barbie doll. I heard them loud and clear, but I knew my husband wouldn't. I decided not to tell him Wayne's secret.

I went uptown and bought two Barbie outfits and put them in the box springs with my son's doll. I taped a note to his gift that said, "I love you, Wayne, no matter what. Love, Mom."

Save Dave

THERE ARE PRAYERS FOR YOU.

Everyone thinks you're on the wrong path. But you're just cocky and know exactly who and what you are.

The church is organizing a fundraising carnival for you and a few other troubled teens in the congregation. They want to send you away to an expensive school with a more Christian environment.

The Miller family has access to a snow-cone machine.

The choir director is setting up a face-painting booth.

Pastor Ringwald confesses that he's a magician and will perform tricks.

There'll be a ring toss, balloon popping, and target practice games.

Sandy Culper has a big idea: her husband has the carpentry plans to build a dunking booth from scratch.

"We should put Dave in the booth. People would pay good

money to dunk him," you hear her chuckle at the church picnic your mom forced you to go to.

Everything's falling into place for what some are calling the "Save Dave" Carnival. The last weekend of July is chosen to raise the money to send you away.

You tell your mom you don't want to sit in the dunking booth.

"You have to," she says. "You're the biggest draw of all the fallen kids."

What?

Your dad instructs you to paint a sign: DUNK THE PUNK.

Dunk you, Dad.

The day of the carnival is very hot. There's already a line of men paying fifty cents a ball to get a crack at you.

You suit up in your skimpy Speedo from swim team.

Up first is that *nice-little-Jesse-from-the-hardware-store*.

"You're going down, Dave?" he says at you as he hurls a ball at the bull's eye.

Ball one misses.

Ball two misses.

You can't help noticing that *nice-little-Jesse-from-the-hardware-store* touches his crotch a lot. He adjusts his crotch to the right with his left hand. You look him right in the eye as he hurls the third ball at your cage.

Jesse is mad. You didn't do anything to him, but he's really shaken that he hasn't dunked you yet.

Maybe you have some power after all.

Up next is Richard. He played football with your big brother a few years ago in high school. You've always liked him from afar (liked him … and liked his big arms.)

Three balls fit easily in his big hand. He's wearing a tight tank top and you can see every muscle in his arms as he pitches the ball at you.

The first ball misses.

Richard smiles at you and winds back to throw his second ball. It's not a friendly smile. It's a crocodile smile like he wants to kill you.

Kill you … or maybe fuck you.

He adjusts his ample crotch with his big hand before he throws again—adjusts to the right just like Jesse.

The second and third balls miss, too.

Richard hands a twenty-dollar bill to the ball keeper.

A gang of sweaty guys are circling to watch Richard dunk you. Big, dumb apes just like him. They're patting Richard on the back and cheering him on.

"Get him."

"Dunk him good."

"Get him wet."

"Show him you mean business."

"Let's make a man out of him."

Sitting dry as a bone on your very own dunking board, you've become an object. A challenge. A prize.

Maybe Richard killing you or fucking you wouldn't be so bad—especially with those big, sexy arms of his. He has a beautiful chest and a slim waist, too.

You don't have to say a word: just shoot him one of your best, shit-eating grins.

He smiles back at you, almost embarrassed.

You're smart and know you don't belong in this small-minded town. He knows that, too.

Richard huffs and puffs: down you go. The water actually feels wonderful. It's almost a relief to finally get dunked.

You climb back up to the seat on your dunking booth. Richard's gang is jumping up and down and high fiving.

You yell at him, "Thanks for that, Dick."

Dick.

He doesn't like Dick and you know it. He goes by the more-Godly name, Richard.

He gives you another *kill-or-fuck look* and dunks you again. You can hear the cheers and jeers underwater. You like it.

You can't wait for Richard to dunk you some more.

Kill me or fuck me, Dick, you think to yourself.

You go down a third, a fourth, and a fifth time for Richard. Every time you get back up, the two of you exchange gritty looks. A connection. A bond. After all, this is just for charity. But is it your charity or his?

Would you rather put your hands around my neck or around my hips, Dick?

You're aroused. You're sporting a hard-on and Richard's throws become steadier, faster, and more meaningful. He passes his balls to his meathead friends so they can dunk you, too. Even *nice-little-Jesse* comes back and finally dunks you. But you focus on Dick as you adjust your Speedo. Sam, Greg, and some guys you don't even know think they're humiliating you each time you hit the water. You want to touch yourself like they do, but you don't dare.

Bring it on, guys.

These apes have dunked you over twenty times in an hour, when you hear, "Dear, Lord. He's getting off on this. Look at him. He's got an erection!"

The party's apparently over. People are fleeing this end of the carnival like you're Godzilla. There're rude grumblings as they walk away from you.

"*Whatever.*"

You'll never forget this hot July day.

Pastor Ringwald approaches you while you're drying off. He's still wearing his dumbass magician's hat.

"Dave, the carnival is no doubt a financial success. Your mother tells me that you've never been baptized. May I baptize you in this dunking booth before you go away to Christian school?"

You tell him no. That has just been taken care of.

Him Outside the Camp

MY FATHER PROCLAIMED LAST SPRING THAT camping would foster good, clean living. There's a Baptist church in the little town nearby or we would have never gone camping. We're spending the summer at Snake Trail Lake before I start my freshman year at a prep school for boys. Dad had a religious guy named Steve bless our truck camper before we could sleep in it.

The campground and its many amenities are all about family, but so far camping is isolating mine. We don't mingle with the other campers, not even the churchgoing ones. Dad goes fishing alone and my mom thinks we don't know that she's reading romance novels under a big oak tree. I stay inside the camper, where I study my Bible. Even when the three of us sit together for Sunday services, the tension is thick. It didn't take long for me to figure out that camping was an alternative to my parents getting a divorce.

More than once this summer, the quiet strain was cut by my

mom and dad taking walks in the woods late at night when they think I'm asleep. I hear scriptures and screaming until the wee hours of the morning. I wish I could do something to help as I listen to my father berate my mother.

Every Thursday afternoon, Mom gets the camper all to herself. She's sitting and brushing her hair as Dad and I ride our bikes into town for provisions. It's a twenty-minute trip to the grocery store; then we typically grab a long lunch and watch TV at the nearby diner. I love having time alone with my dad. However, today he waves me past the grocery store and I follow him to the hardware store.

"Stay out here," he tells me.

Dad comes out of the store with a brand-new Black and Decker electric drill and a small paper bag. He has an ungodly grimace on his face and I'm afraid to ask him what's going on. I was looking forward to our weekly lunch but he quickly leads me back to the lake instead. We've only been gone an hour. I'm suspicious as we park our bikes several feet away from the usual spot.

"Son, please pray with me." I oblige, but I don't really know what I'm praying for this time.

I hang back as he carries the drill toward our camper, where he unwraps it and plugs it into our campsite's designated outlet. Dad takes a long piece of wood from the campfire area and starts drilling it to one side of the camper door with very long screws.

I realize now that Mom must still be inside the camper, and Dad doesn't want her to get out. Loud scriptures and screaming are heard as he starts moving things out of the way and unblocks the truck's wheels. He reaches into the cab of the truck and releases the emergency brake. *I pray to Jesus Christ my Lord and Savior* as Dad walks up behind the camper and starts pushing it with all his might. He has to rock it back and forth a bit, but it finally starts to roll directly toward the lake. I must help my mother, but Dad catches me by my shirt and locks me in a bear hug.

The camper takes out a few small trees as it gains speed down the hill. It topples off the cliff and tips over on its side as it lands in the lake with a horrendous crash. Our blessed camper now rests in shallow water and does not move.

I forgo the dirt path and slide right down the hill through the brush to the rocky shore. Mom has managed to climb out that tiny window above the sink and is sitting on the outside of the toppled camper in nothing but her underwear. A long-haired man with a beard crawls out the window behind her. He's wearing sandals and Mom's long white bathrobe. He looks like Jesus to me. Mom hysterically pats the cross at her throat as the man comes ashore and runs away. My father is at the top of the cliff on his knees, praying. This is way too much for me to handle.

I don't remember how I got into the back of my grandma's car. What's she doing at Snake Trail Lake?

"You're going to stay with me for a while."

I didn't see my mom and dad anywhere, just lots of other people talking to each other. Yet no one's talking to me.

Grandma makes me nervous when we get to her house. She does a lot of whispering into the phone but won't tell me where my parents are or if they're okay. Instead, she sermonizes me constantly about marriage and lies and fornication.

"There's great concern for your spiritual wellbeing," she tells me.

I would appreciate it more if she told me what's really going on.

My parents finally show up. Dad says what happened at the lake was an accident. He makes me angry beyond my years.

"Are you and Mom getting a divorce?" I ask my dad.

"No. But you never have to go camping again."

"Isn't a divorce better than murder?"

"It's complicated, Son."

By now, I've completely lost my faith, but my parents are just lost. Dad still needs the church and a book of rules to guide him. I don't.

I tell my parents that *I denounce the Lord Jesus Christ* and I don't want to go to that religious school this fall, but they give me no choice. Dad's desperate to put things back exactly the way they were before Snake Trail Lake.

But I notice my mother doesn't wear her cross anymore. And she's stopped hiding her romance novels.

Swimmer's Ear

I SWIM TOO MUCH.

There's water stuck in my right ear and it hurts. I tilt my head to the right, hoping gravity will drain me. Frustrated, I cup my two hands over my ears and create a suction trying to shake it loose. I open my mouth wide like a yawn. Nothing works.

People talk to me, but I can't hear them. I just see them staring at me and moving their lips. When you can't hear What's going on in the world, you don't know what to say.

I say nothing.

It's all a foreign language.

It hurts.

My dad comes up behind me in the kitchen and startles me. He grabs my shoulders and whispers into my left ear,. "I have an idea. Come into the living room." His breath rattles the chlorine-bleached hair that hangs over my good ear. I don't trust my dad. He comes and goes from my life depending on how he and Mom are getting along. He's loud: round and obnoxious. He hits Mom and she fights back. He slapped me a few times at Christmas, too, but today Dad seems extra sensitive to me and my swimmer's ear. I'm uneasy.

My father sits down in his oversized easy chair and spreads his legs a bit.

"Kneel down in front to me," he says.

"What?"

"I'm not going to hurt you. Kneel down and put your head in my lap. I'm going to work on that ear for you."

I do as he says, slowly lowering myself and presenting my right ear to my dad. I face away and try to distract myself with the images on the TV. It's a cowboy show. He loves his cowboy shows.

My good ear is on my dad's left thigh. Now it's really hard to hear. I'm alone in my head: helpless, no sound.

Dad gently strokes my hair away from my bad ear and I see he has a black bobby pin in his hand. He places one hand on my forehead and slowly penetrates my ear canal with the bobby pin.

This is dangerous. You're not supposed to stick anything in your ear, but I let him.

Dad begins to swirl the pin around inside my head and I feel myself leave my body. The smell of his horrible aftershave becomes strong and sweet. His lap gets warmer. My flesh and blood take me to heaven, yet I don't want in.

It feels good.

The pin scrapes inside my ear and my entire body stretches for miles like a cat's. The sensation rattles me to my core, and I moan with relief.

"How does that feel?" Dad asks.

"Good," I answer, "but my ear isn't unplugged yet."

"Do you want me to keep going?"

"Yes. I do."

My father and I have never been this close. I feel warm jets of electricity all over my body as he continues to twirl the bobby pin in my ear. It's strangely comforting. Yet, I'm damaged by the situation. It's wrong. I'm waiting for something bad to happen to me. Dad could go too deep and ruin me for life.

My head's lumbering on dad's lap like a clumsy log ride. In a dull climax, I feel a pop. A trail of liquid travels down my throat and I swallow over and over and over. The blockage in my ear has broken free. I can hear again.

I hear a gunfight on the television.

I roll off of my dad's lap onto the floor at his feet.

"Works every time," Dad says. "A pin is better than one of those swabs. Don't tell your mother I stuck a pin in your ear. She'll have my hide."

"I won't," I say.

My ear might be unplugged, but I'm coated in confusion. I yearn for more from my dad. It's not just about my ear. When he hit me at Christmas, I knew I was alive. I had his undivided attention, but it hurt.

This whole summer has been different. My body's changed since last year. Everyone looks at me and remarks on how much better my swimsuit fits and how good I look with a tan. Even the lifeguards stop and look me up and down. I've grown taller, but I feel small and empty.

I think Dad wants to fuck me. He looks at me the wrong way every day. Since the swimmer's ear, he tries to touch me—but I won't let him. Mom and I don't want a cowboy around the house. No more gunfights on the TV.

I need a strong man to love me. I love him and I hate him at the same time.

I stopped swimming this summer and Dad went away. Mom said it's for good this time. And that's okay with me.

The Sissy Test

"FAG" IS A BAD WORD AT your school, so the guys call you a "nancy-boy" so they won't get in trouble.

Yet it's weird. The two most popular girls in your eighth-grade class are both named Nancy.

You spy on the Nancys.

"Are you ready, Nancy?" Nancy X asks. She's holding her friend's arm down on the desk.

Nancy X begins to quickly rub a pencil eraser back and forth on the skin of Nancy Y's delicate forearm. She winces in pain. You watch from across the room in complete awe as a nasty wound appears: a mark of bravery and popularity. *The Sissy Test* is complete. Nancy X and Nancy Y were already close, but now they are bonded like sisters.

You watch as The Sissy Test becomes an epidemic in the final weeks of eighth grade: five girls are suspended for hurting each other trying to be like the Nancys. They're all willing to experience pain to be popular.

And so are you, nancy-boy.

The irony of The Sissy Test is clear. You know you're a big sissy, but you don't know what to do about it. You're being crucified for being gay even though you haven't had sex with anyone yet. You can't deny your attraction to your male classmates, but the crude labels hurt you. You want badly to be popular. Or at least liked.

You don't have a close friend to administer The Sissy Test, so you decide to give it to yourself. Back and forth the pencil eraser digs into your forearm, but the experience isn't what you thought it would be. None of the girls in your class described the euphoria you're experiencing. With each scrape on your arm, the desecration sets you free. You can't control anything in your life, but this you can control. The pain of The Sissy Test cancels out all the emotions of being queer.

The relief is short lived.

Once the wound scabs over you're still broken.

"What happened to your arm?" your mom asks.

"I got burnt at school," you answer.

"That isn't from that Sissy Test I heard about at your school, is it?"

"No. That's just for girls," you reply.

But you can't wait to try it again. Wounding yourself takes over your every thought. You shift from pencil erasers to nails to any other sharp objects you can find. Your whole day revolves around The Sissy Test. How can something so rabid and bloody bring you such solace?

Admit it. You're addicted to self-mutilating. By the first day of your freshman year at Robinson High School, you've got marks all over your body.

The Nancy's have long forgotten about The Sissy Test over

the summer. It's ninety degrees outside and you sit behind Nancy X and Nancy Y in third period Latin class, hiding your arms with long sleeves.

"Okay, Latin to English: what does '*Vi veri universum vivus vici*' translate to?" Mr. White asks the class.

"By the power of truth, I, a living man, have conquered the universe," Nancy Y answers.

All the girls swoon over Mr. White. His good looks don't escape you, either. He's tall and muscular with a beautiful, trustworthy face. His thick blond hair is parted on the side and his teeth are perfect and white. You could love and marry a man like him if you didn't hate yourself so much.

But your heart sinks when you spot two messy scars on his wrists peeking out from his long-sleeved shirt. It makes sense now that he too always wears a long-sleeved shirt. It takes one to know one.

You can tell those scars are self-inflicted. The shape and the bumpy ridges are a dead giveaway. You stand in line at his desk with all the better students so you can ask a fake question and get a better look at them. They're the jagged and mean-looking type that come from really slicing and digging at your flesh. You know he would have to be very determined to mess his wrists up like that. More than likely, he wanted to kill himself.

Admit it. You're obsessed with his scars. Once you see them, you can't see anything else in front of you. Deeper and deeper you dig into your own flesh with a nail, or that file, or your favorite scissors. Cutting isn't helping like it used to and you're tearing yourself up inside and out.

It's impossible for you to imagine that the beautiful and well-liked Mr. White could ever be troubled enough to hurt himself or want to die. Yet there's a sick and guilty comfort in the possibility that he could be just like you. You always assumed that no one on earth who would understand how you feel. Maybe he does.

Admit it. You've fallen in love Mr. White. It's not a love that's romantic. Or a love like you have for your mom or a friend. It's a love that comes from fear. A love from trust, whether mutual or not. A love in your heart that really matters too much.

There might be something more to learn from your favorite teacher.

"All right class, pop quiz. Everyone, take out a piece of paper. First, you will conjugate the following verbs," Mr. White announces.

The verbs don't mean much. You haven't been paying attention in class for weeks and you know you're going to fail Mr. White's test. You sit undone in his third period Latin class.

Admit it. You're raw. You just don't have any skin left and you need help.

The bell rings and class is over. You quickly write a message on your test to your teacher.

"... to save, saved, saves, saving—I need your help. I cut myself on purpose in order to feel something. Save me."

Sunday Drive

My son changed everything in one day.

I want to change it back.

He told me about something sick that happened to him. His mom and I didn't know. We are still shocked to know about what happened to our boy fifteen years ago. If he'd told me when all that stuff was going on, I would've taken care of it right there and then.

He told me, "Dad, that was a long time ago. Don't do anything stupid."

I've got a plan.

I've waited patiently all week for today: Sunday. My wife's at a baby shower all afternoon and my son is with his "goth" friends. I've got the house all to myself. I'm not sure I can go through with this, but I've got to do what's best for everybody.

It's one o'clock: time for me to take some serious action. I gently slide the closet door open in the spare bedroom and reach up to the top shelf. I stick my shaky hand under the bottom blanket and pull out my dad's old Smith and Wesson handgun. The gun's beautiful: a family heirloom that *my dad* gave to me before he passed away twenty years ago.

I haven't fired a gun since I was in Iraq. I swore I would never fire one ever again unless I really had to. The taste of killing's still burned in my memory. Now the image of that sick man touching my son—my little boy—wounds me deeply. It rips me to shreds every day to think about it. I need to rest my mind once and for all.

I pull the gun out of its holster and hold it. It's very elegant; a thing of beauty. I love the power if offers: the ability to change everything for the better. A man's got to be ready to protect his family, so it's always loaded. There's plenty of extra bullets in the box nearby. I'm prepared for anything.

I pack the gun and the box of bullets in a paper sack and go to my truck. I pull out of the gravel driveway on to the dirt road and head to town. It's a big day. This is the most important trip I've ever taken.

It really happened to my son.

It was real.

He's a very emotional person. He takes after his mother that way. I've watched him turn into the kind of young man I don't understand. I still love my boy and I want to understand him. We're two very different people and it's destroying our relationship. I try to wrap my head around my son's issues—all his dark thoughts and ideas. His dyed-black hair and the black clothes are bad enough. It's the Satanic music and all his angry poetry that scare me the most. He claims he's just being himself. I understand that teenagers rebel, but I'm not going to watch this go from bad to worse.

He said to me last week, "Leave me alone, Dad. I just gotta do what I gotta do."

I know now I was too soft on my boy. He used to have yellow colored hair and the face of an angel. I probably set him up to get touched by that monster. I allowed my son to be a victim and now he's full of rage. I should've kept a better eye on him. I can't let my son think that I don't care.

This Sunday drive is what I decided I've got to do. I hope he understands someday.

The dusty roads are turning to pavement as I get into town. There's a knot in my throat—the same sensation I had when I was a soldier in heavy combat.

My hands are sore. I've been gripping the steering wheel of my truck so hard that I feel like I'm about to tear it out of the dashboard. My son's molester is still living in town in the same house after all these years. It makes me sick to think of all of the other little boys and girls he's no doubt ruined since he took my son's innocence.

Do the right thing.

Be a man. Do the right thing. Fix the problem.

I pull my truck up to the building and get out with my sack of bullets and the gun. I slowly walk up the sidewalk to the porch steps of the old house on Cross Street that was converted into the town's sheriff's office.

"How can I help you?" the sheriff asks.

"My name is Bob Coates," I say. "My boy was molested by Dave Drennen fifteen years ago. I want to file a report about it. I also need you to take this sack away from me before my son hurts himself or I go to Drennen's house and kill that sonofabitch."

My Cousin Deborah

I HAD ALL THE DOORS AND windows in the house wide open. Three fans were strategically placed about in an effort to circulate the air around.

It did no good.

I wasn't sure why I agreed to put a home perm in my sixteen-year-old niece's hair on the hottest day of the summer, 1980.

Penny bounced into the house and my knees almost buckled. She had brought our fifteen-year-old cousin, Deborah with her. I hadn't seen Deborah in several years. I was absolutely stunned to see Deborah. She had gotten so tall and beautiful.

"Hey, Janet, Debbie wants a perm, too," Penny announced and launched right back into their fast girl-talk without skipping a beat. Teenage girls take everything for granted. I was quickly reminded of when I was fifteen years old and all that crazy gibber-jabber.

Penny was my sister's girl, born without her father around. There had been many stepfathers. I had as many marriages as my sister. So had our mother. Bad choices run in our family.

"Who wants to go first?" I asked.

"I will," said Penny. She sat down with the home perm kit and took out all the pieces and placed them on the kitchen table.

The girls kept talking and talking about boys. Penny was no stranger to the older boys who smoked and drank and had their own cars. Penny never really had a curfew and could pass for a twenty-five-year-old with her ample breasts.

Despite being cousins, I never got to know Deborah very well. I quickly figured out from the girl's conversation that my cousin was much calmer than my niece. Cousin Deborah liked boys her own age strictly from afar. I gathered that she never had a boyfriend and was still a virgin. She emulated everything Penny said and did and obviously aspired to be more like Penny but didn't have the confidence yet. That concerned me greatly.

"Here, let me help you, Janet," Deborah said.

"Thank you, honey," I said, sweat running down my back. Her attention barely left Penny's boy-crazy chatter as she began methodically handing me the perm rods, one by one, on my cues.

Cousin Deborah had a past that she didn't know about: she had been adopted by my Uncle Henry and Aunt Emily when she was a baby. The whole extended family wondered when she would be told the truth. The girl had been raised well by Henry and Emily, but she was unwittingly living in a lie. My uncle sternly warned everyone in the family not to spill the beans about Deborah's adoption or there would be serious consequences.

I got Penny's hair all rolled on the rods and it was Deborah's turn. She traded places with Penny at the table. As she sat in the chair with her back to me, I almost passed out. A wave of hot air hit me. The stench of the perm solution got much stronger.

My hands were very tired as I finished rolling Deborah's hair. Reeking of perm solution, the girls set the egg timer and ran off to watch TV.

I would never want to be fifteen again.

A girl never forgets being labeled a slut.

The timer dinged.

The girls went to the bathroom and rinsed each other's hair. I watched them pull their own perm rods out. They giggled and admired their wet, new curls in the bathroom mirror.

"Now don't wash your hair or go swimming for a few days or the perm won't hold," I warned as they bounced toward the front porch to leave.

"We won't, Janet. Thanks for perming my hair," Deborah said, looking me square in the face.

I froze on the hottest day of the summer.

I couldn't ignore it any longer. Looking back at me were the eyes of a cute young guy who picked me up one Friday night by the side of the road when I was fifteen. The night after Thanksgiving, 1964.

"You're welcome, Deborah," I said. "Please be careful."

Truant

ALONE AT HOME, I'M A TEACHER. My bedroom is my classroom.

"Welcome, class, to your first day of the 1978 to 79 school year," I say to twenty-five paper recipe cards. Each 3x5 card serves as a pretend school desk and has a pretend student's name on it. The recipe cards are arranged on my twin bed as a classroom seating chart. I took all the blank cards I could find in the kitchen drawer.

Mom put a large chalkboard on the wall in my bedroom that I use to teach my class. As the teacher, I'm in control of the room. My voice is polished and all my students love me. Not at all like how I feel being a real student in the real seventh grade.

One can tell a good teacher from a bad teacher by how neat their grade book is. The numbers, letters, or check marks next to a student's name tells of the past and can predict the future. Students are at my mercy and that of a simple, spiral-bound notebook with specific lines and boxes designed just for a teacher.

Using a ruler, I have always drawn my own grade book with all the lines in the right place using blank typing paper and a marker. But it's hard to keep the lines crisp and equal. It's fake and doesn't give me the authority I crave. I'm no longer happy with my homemade grade book. I need a better grade book to be a better teacher.

The stores uptown sell all kinds of ledgers, journals, and notebooks, but the spaces are not right for a teacher. I can't take an accountant's ledger and turn it into a teacher's grade book. That's not good enough.

Middle school just keeps sucking for me. All the snotty remarks and prods. I get smaller and smaller in my class. I need another sick day, so the nurse has arranged for my grandmother to pick me up from school before lunch. Asthma is my excuse again. My mom will get me at my grandparents' house after her work's done at the factory. Grandpa and Grandma live two blocks away from Lincoln Grade School. I went to that school until the fifth grade. It was better back then.

I'm not really sick. I can tell Grandma knows it.

"I'm going for a walk to catch my breath," I tell Grandma as I get out of her station wagon. She watches me saunter down the driveway toward my old grade school but says nothing. She has no idea what I have planned. I'm not sure I do, either.

Truancy. I looked it up in the dictionary. This isn't that. I'm absent from my middle school, yet I'm sitting on the steps of the grade school across town. I'm the invisible boy. Our little town doesn't have a truancy officer anyways.

I want to be at home, in my room …teaching in my bedroom classroom where I'm respected. I miss my recipe card students.

I kick the bad kids out of my classroom.

"Detention for you, young man!" I say out loud.

I give good grades to my good students.

A's and B's.

"I'm so proud of you and your work."

The lunch bell at Lincoln Grade School startles me: I hear the students file onto the playground behind the building. I get up from the concrete steps and march right up to the front door of the school and walk in. Like I'm a teacher. Did I mention that my mom went to this school, too, in the 1940s?

There's an echo inside the halls of my old grade school that I miss. The marble floor and high ceilings haven't changed a bit. The horrible middle school I go to now is very modern with bright colors and carpeted floors. It was built in 1972.

All the classrooms are empty. I duck into my old second grade classroom and look out the window at the little kids on the playground still on their lunch break.

I take the stairs to the second floor and enter my old fourth grade classroom. I see an open grade book in the center of the teacher's desk. It's spiral bound like they all are. The paper is unique: pale green with black lines. I'm in awe of the thick green cardboard cover with its bumpy, textured feel.

I sit down at the teacher's desk and carefully thumb through the book. The left margin of each page is perforated and folded back—one page per subject: English, Math, Spelling, Social Studies, Science. Each piece of paper swings over and lines up perfectly with the list of students' names, hand-printed by the teacher in blue ink. The school year has just started. There are barely any marks in the book. It's practically brand new.

"Detention for you, young man!" I say out loud to the empty classroom.

I fold the grade book closed and tuck it into my jacket. I make my way to the next classroom and take another grade book right off the fifth-grade teacher's desk. The bell rings and startles me again. Lunch is over and I hear the students coming up the stairwell. I quickly duck into the music room.

I'm scared. I don't want to get caught. The music room is my bunker while I wait for the kids to get settled back into their classrooms. I pull the grade books out of my jacket and examine them while I wait. The names and grade are all unknown to me, but both books are beautiful: linear, clean, artistic. The two teachers had thoughtfully judged and documented each student work with symbols that were as important as brushstrokes in a painting.

Truancy doesn't occur to me. I must paint my own picture of judgment and grades.

Once clear, I find myself again on the front steps of Lincoln Grade School. My chest is suddenly heavy like I described to the school nurse earlier this morning. I'm jumpy like the time I ate five candy bars, one after another.

I quickly make my way back to my grandparents' house.

"How are you feeling?" Grandma asks.

"Better," I answer.

"The fresh air probably did you some good," she says without taking her eyes off her silly soap opera. *The Young and the Restless*, I think.

Mom picks me up after work. There's barely an exchange between Mom and Grandma about my supposed asthma attack. They both know of my struggles in the seventh grade. That's unlikely to change anytime soon.

At home, safe in my bedroom, I waste no time tearing out all the written-on pages of the stolen grade books. It feels good to throw them away. I just erased two whole classrooms without remorse. There's plenty of blank pages left. Now I can relax and fill the grade books with my own grades and check marks. Vivid, perfect, and mine.

Eighty-Five Days

I GUESS YOU COULD SAY IT was planned. The UPS man brought me the package while I was still in my nightgown, but I was ready. Inside the small shipping crate was a custom-made little baby boy named Lyle, painstakingly airbrushed and rooted by an artist so he would look like the real thing.

His skin, eyes, and hair were a perfect blend of mine and "Van's." I call the man from the van "Van" now. He wasn't going to be around to help me raise the baby and I refused to answer any questions about him. My focus has always been on being a good mom.

Once I had Lyle, I put my family and friends on the back burner: no calls or visits. If they didn't understand what was going on, so be it.

I believed in Lyle from the moment I opened the box. I remember swaddling him in my arms and taking him into the spare bedroom that I just turned into a nursery. I had painted the walls and made new curtains. The crib, changing table, and rocking chair were from Ikea. A nice young man helped me load the stuff into the truck I rented. People are always so helpful when you're shopping for baby stuff.

In the beginning, I bonded with my baby boy twenty-four hours a day. It was a rewarding experience for me to bathe him and change his diapers. I loved to sing cute little songs. There was a tiny closet full of tiny clothes. I had plenty of knit booties in happy colors on hand.

The point of Lyle was to appear normal. I paid special attention when I put him in his car seat, or when I went out with him in his stroller. One day at the park, an older woman came up to admire my baby. She cooed at him (which I wanted) but she saw the paint and rooting and gave me a dirty look. It didn't register in my head. The same thing started happening in the grocery store every time we went. I wasn't exactly pretending; I really did believe I was a mom and learned to block out anything to the contrary.

Things were always rough for me at night. I couldn't bear to put Lyle down in his new crib so he slept beside me in my queen-sized bed. I could hear him cry and it made me cry. It was soothing in an *if a tree falls in the forest* kind of way. My son was already teaching me new things.

I know you think I'm crazy. I can own that now. The things in my head didn't always connect or make sense to me. I think it's good for me to finally share my story.

You see, when I found out I was pregnant two years ago, I went into denial. Only recently did I look at a calendar and figure out that I'd carried Van's child for eighty-five days before I got an abortion. The next thing I knew, I was pretending to be a mom to Lyle: a doll. I guess I needed to have the baby I didn't have. I got lost in the "what ifs."

It took a while, but I started seeing Van in the doll's rooted eyelashes and glass eyes. I saw the face of the man who beat me and raped me in that van. That must be why I bought a doll that looked like Van, but I didn't know that yet.

Something blocked me from getting angry at Van. I was hollow and confused right though the abortion, which I barely remember. There was no rage or any grieving and things weren't getting any better. I actually thought for a long time that I hadn't had abortion; I thought I'd imagined it.

You know what's funny? When I was a little girl, I didn't even like dolls. I was going through this rewind and redefine process. Does any of this make sense?

So one day, I caught myself squeezing the doll's head without really knowing it. Air came out of a seam around its neck—just like Van choked and tried to squeeze the air out of me. I became completely furious with the baby, and it felt *right*. I woke up with a doll and a room full of baby furniture. All of a sudden, I could feel everything I didn't get to feel before.

I remember Van spitting on his hand before he raped me. It was disgusting and I threw up in my mouth when he did that. Standing there in the nursery, I almost threw up on the baby doll.

I went from loving the doll with all my might one minute to wanting to kill the doll the next. Suddenly I was this angry woman I had never met. I went over to the window and ripped the baby curtains down as hard as I could and left the nursery. I was done with all the denial and pretending that men put me through.

That's my only explanation for that period of my life.

An explanation isn't an apology, is it? I don't apologize for anything I did.

It was easy to donate all the baby furniture to a woman's shelter and repaint the room. But I was left with this doll. I couldn't just throw it away. I didn't want it to go to a thrift store where it would be given a price tag and thrown on a shelf with a bunch of other dolls. There was more to this doll than that.

This doll needed to be reborn.

I carefully dressed him in the best outfit he had and placed him in a discreet box with a blue ribbon. I drove to a nearby firehouse and secretly placed the box on the front steps. I was sure they'd know what to do.

The Bohemian Medusa

VERDI'S *AIDA* BELLOWED ON THE STRANGER'S iPod. The volume was so loud he didn't hear Sally's battle cry.

"WHA WA WHAA," is what her scream sounded like to him outside the opera in his headphones.

His confused face—with perfectly sculpted eyebrows—twisted before he landed one strong defensive blow to her head. There were no witnesses to the attack. Blood immediately began collecting like an hourglass in her angry, twitching eyeballs.

"There's some serious bruising above her ear: blunt force trauma. I'll betcha she has a brain-bleed," the paramedic whispered with concern to his partner. The slender young woman had been blinded, but she could still hear them talking about her. A small crowd had gathered as she was quickly taken away in an ambulance to Robinson Hospital.

Her long dreadlocks were shaved off for surgery and given back to her in a trash bag. An aide opened the bag and put

Sally's hand inside so she could feel. The hairs had spun themselves into tight sticks like branches on a tree. Heavy beads were still on the pieces of hair that used to frame her face.

Sally remained sightless, despite the emergency surgery. The trauma left her with amnesia; the memory of her assault was vague. Hadn't the man who blinded her worn Polo or Prada or some sort of overpriced, preppy garb? What was his weapon? She was paranoid, yet needed help fitting the pieces together.

A receiving line of old allies rallied around her in the hospital.

"A bunch of dirty lesbians," the head nurse called them as they entered the ward.

Still bandaged, Sally begged each of her friends to tell her what had happened. But they didn't know. They weren't there.

"Weren't there some details in the newspaper? Anything?" she asked.

Nothing. She would interrogate her friends until they left angry. Eventually, the visits just stopped.

The days and nights of darkness alone in her hospital room were torture. She only knew the dawn of each day by the sickening smell of the eggs and bacon offered her by a cafeteria aide.

"I don't eat meat or dairy," she snapped.

Sally lay in her bed contemplating, not ready to surrender. She worried she would become irrelevant despite her strong voice and ethics. A staff counselor was there to help her sort out her possibilities, but she was more focused on her advocacy than her rehabilitation.

On the last day of her stay in the hospital, a familiar smell of cologne wafted into her room. A sturdy, baritone voice said her name.

"Sally?" he bellowed.

"Yes."

"My name is Felix. I'm the director of musical performance over at the junior college."

"Do you know me?"

"Well, no. Not really," the man answered timidly. "I'm so sorry about what happened to you. I came here this afternoon to apologize, make peace. Listen, I don't know how to say this other than to just say it."

Sally got chills as she heard the man nervously shift his feet on the floor. "I'm afraid that I'm the man who did this to you. I hit you on the head."

Sally rose up out of her hospital bed as an angry Phoenix ready to avenge her honor.

"You're the one who blinded me? You're the person who ruined my life? " she asked.

"Yes … but let me explain. I had my iPod on and couldn't hear you. You just came out of nowhere. Your dreads were flying all over the place and hitting me in the face. You looked crazy and I just acted on impulse," Felix said with perfect resonance.

"Get the fuck out of my room before I kill you! People like you make me sick! Go on! You better get out of here! NURSE! GET THIS MONSTER OUT OF MY ROOM!" screamed Sally.

She grabbed the bag of her old hair and hurled it at the door as Felix spun on his fancy shoes and fled her room.

Within minutes, Sally felt a tiny prick to her vein. The nurse hummed a soft tune as the medicine calmed her nerves.

"It's all right now, Sally. Relax. We won't let him come back to bother you again," the nurse said.

"Ohhhhh … fuck," Sally said under her breath.

"What's wrong?"

"I wish I'd asked him what happened that day. I need to know why that monster did this to me."

"Didn't anyone tell you?"

"No, I still don't know everything."

The nurse leaned in and stroked the stubble on the young woman's head.

"A paramedic told everyone in the ER the whole story. He said you screamed at the opera guy outside the Walmart because he was wearing a full-length mink coat. You scared him and he blinded you in self-defense."

"What … what did he hit me with? What'd he use?" Sally asked her nurse.

"Well, apparently he was carrying a two-liter bottle of tonic water in one of those plastic shopping bags: the kind with the handles. He told the paramedics that he swung the bag around and nailed you with one good swing."

"What?"

"Yeah … he left a message at the nurse's station just now to tell you that he made a thousand-dollar contribution to PETA in your name."

Mr. Blue

MARK SLOWLY WADDLED TO THE 7-ELEVEN across from Robinson Hospital after his doctor appointment. He coughs as he pays for some smokes and a single red rose sold in a protective plastic sheath. Today is his thirtieth wedding anniversary. His lovely wife deserves more, but they are on a strict budget.

Beeeep, Beeeep, Beeeep, Beeeeep.

The driver lowers the wheelchair ramp so he can board the #7 bus home. The passengers frown at the four-hundred-pound man as he lumbers down the aisle to find a seat. There's a collective sigh of relief when he gets off at the stop in front of his house.

When her husband walks into the living room, Melissa's quick to ask how his appointment went.

"There's nothing to worry about. The doctor told me to take some Tums and try to relax," Mark says.

He gives his wife the rose and playfully touches her breasts.

"Happy anniversary, honey. I look forward to more of *these* when you get home later."

"Frisky? What's gotten into you?" Melissa asks.

"You're a wonderful woman. You've made me very happy all these years," he answers.

Melissa is giddy for the first time in months. Her suspiciously amorous husband gives her a pat on the ass as she leaves the house for work. She looks great in her waitress uniform. He's glad that she's maintained her figure all these years.

With the house to himself, Mark checks out the Craigslist personals. He heard about Craigslist from his nephew at a family barbecue.

"You can get fucked or get a blow job any time of the day or night. It's also a cheap way to get a bunch of Viagra or weed," the nephew confessed.

Mark is still amused to learn that Viagra is referred to as "Mr. Blue" on the site—an attempt to fool the police. The erectile dysfunction medication is big business and requires a prescription to obtain lawfully.

After another cigarette, he places a personal ad looking for some triangular blue pills. Within an hour, Mr. Blue is delivered right to his door by a jittery kid with two-tone hair and tight jeans.

Watching TV from his broken recliner, Mark glares at the envelope of pills and waits for Melissa to come home. The same commercial prods him over and over during his shows.

"Ask your doctor if your heart is healthy enough for sex," the voice-over says.

Truthfully, Mark knows he isn't healthy enough for sex. He lied to Melissa. His doctor told him this morning that if his heart didn't kill him, the smoking eventually would. It's going to be impossible to hide his cardiovascular disease. There's still plenty of life left for his wife without him dragging her down with breathing tubes and bedpans. He decided even before his doctor's appointment that the best thing for everyone would be for him to kill himself with virile dignity: suicide disguised as love and sex.

At precisely 10:20 p.m., Mark overdoses on his bootleg Viagra and begins flipping through an old porn magazine.

"Honey, I'm home," Melissa says, springing into the living room.

He slides out of his recliner and wobbles over to her as quickly as his ample body will allow. The lovebirds share an anniversary slow dance without music. Melissa hasn't even set her purse down yet.

"I've been thinking about you all day," Melissa confesses with a girlish smile.

"No, I've been thinking about *you.*"

Holding hands, the two go to their bedroom. They awkwardly peel each other's clothes off as they try to kiss each other passionately between Mark's coughs. Melissa sits on the edge of the bed and welcomes her husband's dick in her mouth.

Mr. Blue is working.

Mark wheezes as he runs his hands through his wife's hair. His heart is certainly beating overtime, but he isn't sure if it is from the pills or the possibility of dying soon.

"I love you. I love you," he pants to his wife.

Distracted, she doesn't respond.

Sex feels very good to Mark, but death penetrates his thoughts while Melissa services him.

My wife's going to have to pick out a large coffin for me.

Or maybe she'll just cremate me, burn me up, he thinks as he catches a glimpse of her head bobbing in his crotch.

Mark turns bright red as he slowly lumbers up into the bed on his back. His overwhelmed heart is racing and sweat is flooding out of him. A shocking reflection of himself in the dresser mirror reveals an engorged monster.

I hope she finds another man and remarries. A good man in good health.

Melissa mounts her husband and rides him the best she can.

"I. Love. You," Mark mutters again with breathy gasps. His ears are ringing and veins are popping out all over.

"ILOVEYOUTOOHONEY," Melissa says. Her face is pink and her eyes are watering. She's enjoying herself, but a death montage floods her husband's mind: putting the family dog down; the DC sniper killing all those people back in 2002; did Nelson Rockefeller really die while having sex?

In one last glance at Melissa, she appears to him as an angel. Suddenly he changes his mind. He wants to live but is scared it's too late.

The ticker in his brain shifts: *Fight ... Job ... Win ... Bitch ... Touch. SHOOT.*

He bursts inside his wife, then his brain goes lifeless. His heart stops and there's a moment of peace.

Yet his messy life is still hovering.

After a few beats, he hears a familiar voice.

"Happy anniversary, honey. That was fun," Melissa says with a smile.

Mark struggles to open his eyes. He's alive after all.

I've gotta quit smoking and lose a hundred pounds, he says to himself.

Robinson, IL

NINE A.M., ROBINSON, IL.

A beat-up truck pulls into the parking lot at the Cadillac dealership out by the Dairy Queen.

"We can do this," Becky Collier says to her husband.

"I know. We gotta do this," Ed answers and squeezes his wife's hand.

A salesman wastes no time meeting them outside.

"We'd like to buy one of your new Escalades," Ed tells the salesman.

"Is this a trade-in?"

"No. We're keeping our old truck."

The salesman walks the couple out to the lot and they quickly pick out a brand-new model with all the bells and whistles. The couple test-drives the truck with very little thought.

"We'll take it."

The salesman's surprised at how fast and easy he makes the sale. The Colliers are escorted inside, where the men spend the next two hours hammering out the money with the dealership's financial office while Becky waits outside. It's a tough transaction. They are risking their house and their farm, yet Ed agrees to an $890 a month payment for the next sixty months. He's afraid to tell his wife how much he took out of their account for the down payment.

By noon, Ed drives the brand-new Escalade off the lot with his wife following behind in their old pickup truck.

They meet at McDonald's out by the freeway for a quick lunch. Ed calls to check in with their daughter, Patricia Collier, in Nevada.

"Yes, honey. I got it. We'll keep you posted," he tells her.

Ed and Becky still have a long day ahead of them. Once they finish their value meals, they each get on I-70 separately in their new and old trucks for the ninety-minute drive to Starkville, Illinois. They have an appointment at a seedy place called Stinkie's Auto Mart.

The two trucks pull into the parking lot right on time. Ed and the owner, Stinkie, have been on the phone a lot the last week.

"It's good to finally meet you," Stinkie says.

He takes a long look at the Escalade before the three of them go into his makeshift office. The smell of cheap cigars is enough to make Becky want to throw up.

"Okay, so let me get this straight. You want me to take this brand-new vehicle off your hands for cash without a title?"

"Yes," Ed says. "We'll maintain the financing and make the payments with our bank like nothing happened. You do whatever it is you do with vehicles. If there's ever a problem, we'll report the Cadillac stolen."

"May I ask why you need so much cash?" Stinkie asks after a hefty puff on his cigar.

For the first time all day, the overwrought wife has something to say. She takes over the conversation and fills the room with desperation.

"If you must know, our twenty-two-year-old son, Peter, is transgendered. We need money to pay for her—we call her Patricia now—her sexual reassignment surgery. All the banks refused our loan request. Out of prejudice, I suppose."

Ed turns white as a ghost at his wife's admission. He's afraid she has ruined the deal.

"I'm sorry," he says. "My wife's very frustrated. We just need the money and hope you can help."

Stinkie gets up from his desk and looks out the window.

"This may come as a surprise to you, Mr. and Mrs. Collier, but I'm a pretty open-minded guy," he says. "I don't know much about the whole transgender thing, but my son is gay."

"Oh, really?"

"Yes. He got the shit beat out of him more than once for being gay. It isn't exactly San Francisco around here."

The couple watch Stinkie change from a sketchy dealer into a thoughtful father right before their eyes.

"I love my son no matter what he is," Stinkie says softly.

Becky pulls out a dog-eared notebook with a picture of their daughter on the cover. She tenderly begins sharing letters from doctors and takes the businessman through every details of changing Patricia's gender from male to female.

"She lives in Nevada now. You know it's not safe around here. The money from that new vehicle plus our savings has to be enough for the surgery and to fly us out to be with her when she gets it done."

Stinkie sees tears well up in Becky's eyes.

"I'm very impressed with how organized you are, Mrs. Collier. I would be honored to help your family out," he tells the couple.

The deal is sealed with a handshake: nothing on paper. And like something right out of a movie, Stinkie leaves the room and comes back with a briefcase full of cash. He gives the Colliers a big, smelly bear hug and watches them get into their old pickup with the suitcase. The relieved couple will never see Stinkie or the luxury vehicle again.

Patricia's surgery goes well and payments on the Escalade are always made on time. She helps her parents pay off the loan when she can and thinks she will be ready to come home to Illinois for a visit next Christmas.

The family's forever grateful for the unusual help they got from Stinkie. The clandestine deal he made them helped immensely.

Six months later, there's a new customer at Stinkie's Auto Mart. Chris Johnson drove all the way from Missouri in a shiny new Chevy Silverado he bought from a dealer there just yesterday.

"What can I do for you, Mr. Johnson?" Stinkie asks.

"Well … I heard through a friend that you're a very open-minded businessman, and that you'll wipe a new car for cash. I'm transgender and have been living as a man for a while. My bank won't help me, and I really need the surgery."

"I'm so sorry for your frustration. Please, step into my office, Mr. Johnson," Stinkie responds.

The Miller Family Reunion

A HEATWAVE ENGULFS THE HOMETOWN PAVILION. You're uneasy as you park the car. About sixty relatives are already setting up the food on the picnic tables.

This is your new wife's first Miller Family Reunion. She sits next to you in the car pensively biting her nails. It's been a busy few weeks and she's tired from packing up the apartment. After graduation at the community college, you're leaving Robinson and moving to Chicago so you can finish your bachelor's degree.

"Do I look all right?" she asks.

"You look fine. I like that blouse," you answer. You know that she likes it when you throw a random compliment at her. She's not used to compliments.

You make your wife carry her own covered dish to the event. What she made is a bit "white trash": Twinkies shredded into vanilla pudding with Cool Whip topping. Hopefully nobody notices who brought it and passes judgment. Both of you hope to get through this day without embarrassing yourselves.

"Oh, you're finally here," your mom says.

The chitchat starts. Waves of kin are swarming the picnic like flies.

"Why aren't you introducing Julia to anyone?" your mom whispers.

You don't answer. It's glaringly obvious to your mom that you have absolutely no intention of showing off your new wife. She saves her daughter-in-law from humiliation while you wander over to the food table. You can't help noticing the Twinkie dish is already a big hit.

"This is Julia … Denny's new wife," she says over and over to anyone who will listen.

"Welcome to the family, Julia."

The day is slow and humdrum until you see your Cousin Jeremiah ride into the park on his noisy motorcycle. He made the five-hour trip from Chicago to surprise his parents at the Miller family reunion. No one's seen or heard much of him in the last few years.

Jeremiah's mom and dad run to greet their leather-clad son at his motorcycle. His parents are overjoyed, but there are gasps from other relatives when he takes off his jacket and reveals he's got a plethora of tattoos. Even *your* jaw drops at the sight of his new look. You are the same age, but he's transformed himself into one of those alternative types.

There're mumblings from a few of your hateful uncles.

"He's not a *real* biker, if you know what I mean," Uncle Mic says under his breath. You cringe at his redneck comment.

"This is Julia, Derrick's new wife," your mom announces to your Cousin Jeremiah. "The happy couple is moving to Chicago in a few weeks."

Your wife cautiously shakes the biker's hand.

"I'm sure you will make a lot of new friends in the big city, Derrick," Jeremiah says with a confident grin. His voice hasn't changed a bit. He still sounds like the boy next door.

Your cousin has caught you starring at his sexy tattoos. They're like a messy buffet arranged here and there on his chest, arms, and even his neck. You can't help but notice that some of them are pretty "gay.".

Jeremiah quickly fixes a plate of food for himself. More and more relatives arrive, but he sticks closely to his folks and doesn't mingle. Your wife nervously laughs when she sees a big helping of her Twinkie dessert on his plate.

Aunt Winnie, the obnoxious one, blows a whistle. The Miller family shifts their focus to the far end of the pavilion for some boring family presentation, complete with a podium and enlarged photos. You make your way to the park restroom and have a quick, secret smoke. Jeremiah's the one who taught you to smoke back in middle school and you hope he will follow you there so you two can talk privately. Sadly, he doesn't follow you.

Making your way back to the family, you notice that Jeremiah and his bike are gone. You're disappointed and you take a spot in the back corner of the pavilion by yourself. Your wife's sitting near the front of the crowd with your parents.

Julia has no idea that you are not taking her with you to Chicago. This is definitely the one and only Miller family reunion she will ever attend. It may be your last one, too.

The family sits for over an hour in the hot park shelter and share happy memories. But nobody talks about how Aunt Lucy is a drunk, or how Bobby beats his wife and kids. Everyone knows that Grandpa almost divorced Grandma back in the early 1970s. Nothing like that is being said.

You still love the crazy relatives but wish that someone had the guts to acknowledge that you, Jeremiah, and your Aunt Linda are all gay. Everyone already knows the truth. It would mean a lot if someone spoke up at the family tribute and proclaimed that the three of you are all smart and worthy people. You're just as good as anyone else in the family, despite your sexuality.

Getting out of your parents' house and marrying a woman seemed like the right thing to do a year ago. You didn't know then what you know now. The next step is to get a divorce and finish college so you can follow your dream in a tolerant city. You know you can't be happy married to a woman and living in Robinson. Hopefully your wife will forgive you someday.

After the family tribute is over, your mom puts a small piece of paper in your hand. There's a phone number and email address on it.

"Jeremiah had to leave early, but he wanted me to give this to you. He said to be sure and let him know when you get to town and he can help you and Julia get acquainted with Chicago," she says.

"Thanks, Mom. I'll be sure to call him," you tell her as you put the piece of paper in your pocket.

VOTE

THERE WERE VERY FEW FLYERS UP around the gayborhood and they didn't say much: no date, no time, and no location. The flyers just say VOTE: A NEW GAY DANCE CLUB—COMING SOON. It's rumored to be inspired by Studio 54 back in its heyday—you know, when the bouncer handpicked the hot and important people outside the club. Not everyone will be invited in. It's very exclusive.

The address everyone is passing around is an old Circuit City building out by the mall: an abandoned electronics store from the '90s.

Every fag in the city is in line, all puffed up and ready to party in the suburbs. But it's doesn't feel right. The building's all boarded up and it's obvious nobody's inside. There must be five hundred people in the parking lot and no one has any idea what's going on. But everyone's trying to look hot. I know I am.

There's a commotion and I turn around and see an old

guy coming out of the building with a messenger bag. He's methodically making his way through the crowd, handing out golden tickets. I can tell already that no one over thirty is getting one. He isn't giving tickets to women or fat guys, either. I suck in my belly and march right up to him and smile. He hands me a golden ticket, and I'm so fucking excited I can't stand it. But the old fart doesn't give any of my friends a ticket. Fuck. I hate to leave my friends behind, but this is the chance of a lifetime. I'm sure I'll make new friends inside the club tonight.

There's blaring club music from down the street getting closer and closer. All of a sudden a beat-up school bus painted black with the VOTE logo on the side quickly pulls into the Circuit City parking lot. The door to the bus opens and a hot man steps out of the bus. He's dressed in a form-fitting rubber suit and chauffeur's cap—very cute. The guy is sculpted from head to toe and I would definitely let him fuck me. The crowd goes wild as all of us chosen men with golden tickets climb aboard.

It's very dark in the bus. I can't see a thing. The windows are painted black and there are no seats. We're all crammed together standing up and it's not fun or sexy. There are way too many guys on the bus and it's hot (not in a good way). It smells like piss and cologne in here. Finally, I feel the bus moving, but I have no idea where they're taking us.

Jesus Fucking Christ.

We must have left town or something because it's been over an hour. It feels like we're being driven around in circles.

The bus finally stops and lets us off. We're in a giant warehouse. There's a long row of lockers, like at the gym, and a fleet of handsome men are dressed in these strange, queer

Nazi soldier uniforms: short-shorts, tight tank tops, tall leather boots with a military hat all adorned with the scary swastika. It looks like a *Tom of Finland* scene. You can see the outline of their big dicks through their pants.

The old fart who was handing out the golden tickets reappears, now in full traditional Nazi attire.

"Gentlemen, welcome to VOTE," he announces to the wary crowd. "Here you can party till we kill you. Ha-ha! Woot, Woot!" he says with a scary smile, doing that bouncing, *raise the roof* gesture with his arms up in the air. He looks stupid doing that, but … whatever.

A swell of dance music starts playing loud enough to vibrate the metal warehouse as the queer Nazis instruct us to get naked and put all our shit in the assigned locker with our ticket number on it. My locker is next to last: number two hundred ninety-nine.

All three hundred of us are shuffled naked through a set of double doors by the big-dicked guards. They look kind of mean (in a sexy way). It's a bit of a heady feeling being with this many hot guys. I mean, we were all hand-picked. We're the best of the best, but why are we being herded like cattle?

Okay, it's obvious this is supposed to be some sexy, faux concentration camp scene with a political message: kind of cool, but weird. I like the vibe so far, but it's almost too strange being in line for a haircut and tattoo. I really don't want my hair cut and I can't tell if they are *really* tattooing the guys ahead of me.

No one is saying no to this crazy shit. Can we say no? Where the fuck are we going to go … naked? None of us have our phones and we don't know where we are.

The muscle-barber does a terrible job on my hair and I'll

have to fix it later. And I'm a bit annoyed that the tattoos are real. A small VOTE logo is inked on my arm right where they labeled the Jews during World War II. I always get an erection when I'm getting a tattoo. Something about the vibration and the pain, you know? Sure enough, I get hard while the hot Nazi works on me. I'm not the only one here who's aroused. I'm turned on and very vulnerable at the same time.

I bet I'm getting laid tonight.

After the tat and haircut, we're given uniforms that are a sexy version of what was worn in concentration camps. Think *International Male* Catalog or Nasty Pig brand: tight fitting, short, and shiny. And, of course, there is a sequin pink triangle on the left tit. We're all laughing as we get dressed. It's like a sexy-prisoner-Halloween party.

My hard-on goes away as the guards force us to run through a maze, snapping at us with a riding crop. It kind of hurts, but … whatever. We're rushed into a giant room that takes my breath away. It's the biggest, most elaborate dance club I've ever seen in my entire life.

There's a big archway at the entrance that says CLUB AUSCHWITZ, just like what you see in those black and white documentaries. The place is decorated in very expensive furnishings. Everything is black, red, and white. Lots of velvet, metal, and leather mixed with real barbed wire. There is a long bar, which I assume is an *open* bar since none of us has any money. More hot Nazis with fake-little-Hitler mustaches serve as bartenders. I *need* a drink after all this, so I get in line with the other guys.

Off to the side, there's an enormous dance floor with a glowing swastika built into the floor. In the corner there's a DJ who looks exactly like the real Adolf Hitler in full military garb, spinning more and more amazing tunes. He's very focused and not looking at anyone (thank God).

This is what the weeks of hype around the gayborhood is all about. I can finally relax and start talking with a few cute guys. We laugh and joke about our hair and how strange this place is. But we're lucky enough to get into the hottest new gay club. And it's time to have fun!

Two drinks.

Three drinks.

Four drinks.

There are more hot Nazis walking around with trays of any drug you can imagine. The lights and music are getting more and more intense as the evening goes on. I'm in heaven.

My favorite part: (like a grandfather clock, every fifteen minutes) a go-go cage is lowered over us on the dance floor. Inside there's a slutty "Anne Frank" dancing her ass off. She's the only woman in the club. She looks sadly down at the crowd and puts her index finger over her mouth as if to say, "Shhhhhhhh. Don't tell anyone I'm here." Then her cage disappears back up into the rafters.

"Woot! Woot!"

We're all getting fucked up and frisky. There's touching and feeling all over the place. The dance floor is one big knot of sweaty sex, drugs, and music. A few of the hot Nazis have taken off their uniforms and are joining in. Hands down, this is the most decadent thing I have ever experienced.

I'm making out with three different men when I catch a glimpse of a bunch of old men in conservative suits and ties standing around the dance floor. They're wearing gas masks and holding big Bibles.

What the fuck?

The music is turned off and DJ-Hitler makes a startling announcement over a PA system.

"Gentlemen, it's time for a shower."

A giant burst of a fog envelops the dance floor. The smell is sweet and smooth on my lungs. I feel myself getting sleepy and withering down-down-down to the floor on a pile of men who look just like me.

Asleep.

Awake.

I'm alive. I can tell I'm alive.

I can tell I'm outside. Fresh air. It's cold and windy.

I can tell I'm lying on my side. There's a tingle that starts in my fingers and toes. It shoots through arms and my legs to my chest. It's not unpleasant, just different.

I open my eyes and there's a man a few inches away looking at me and another guy behind him. There are more men behind me, too.

I lift my head and see that I've been stacked into a row of naked men. All the men at VOTE were drugged and placed in a freshly dug trench.

But we all seem to be okay.

Guys are slowly starting to get up and move around, shaking it off.

One of the cute guys I was making out with on the dance floor helps me up. There are no Nazis anywhere. I'm thankful to see the lockers with our clothes starkly placed in a field of nothing a few feet away.

I don't know what to think of VOTE.

I hate the tattoo they gave me. I'll have my tattoo guy cover it up with something better when I get back to the city.

The Pirate-Diva

A DEEP BEAT RATTLES THE DANCE floor at the college town's newest gay bar, *Spun.* Daft Punk blends into Beyonce, then swells into Kylie Minogue.

Hank's a transfer student majoring in opera performance, but he loves all music. Tonight he's a diva dressed up in his own pseudo-*Pirates of the Caribbean* ensemble: bright-red hair, purple leggings, tall boots with a wide cuff, and a white, puffy poet shirt belted at the waist. His nails are painted black, and his eyes are lined just like Johnny Depp's.

The plan is to dance his ass off at *Spun*, but he's five cocktails into the night and nothing's inspired him to move. The DJ finally gets his attention with a mashup of the vintage Adam Ant song *Goody Two Shoes* mixed with Katy Perry's *Roar*. It's a blend of old and new that makes the pirate-diva go crazy.

The sound is intense, and Hank's moves are jarring. He's swinging his arms and head around like a maniac. The pirate-diva likes the fact that everyone's watching him on the dance floor: after all, opera is his major. He's a natural scene stealer and is used to being the center of attention.

Another new mix is spun by the DJ, and Hank begins to dance like an angry windshield wiper. Since he knows people are watching, he adds an extra jerk here and there. He's managed to clear a circle around himself on the dance floor.

What Hank doesn't realize is that the patrons are not watching him with admiration; they're gaping at him in horror. It appears he's been shot in the head. No one actually heard a gunshot, but there's blood flicking off his head.

For some reason, the pirate-diva's unfazed despite what looks like a serious injury. He's keeps dancing with such determination, no one dares stop him: they might get hurt or splattered with blood.

Spun's DJ calls 911 but doesn't kill the music for fear it might create a panic at his disco.

"Maybe he's having some sort of seizure standing-up?" he tells the emergency dispatcher.

By now, Hank's the only one dancing. He pulls out all the stops, thinking he's somehow been granted a solo recital.

The paramedics arrive quickly and stop him mid-groove.

"What's going on? Is everything all right?" he shouts.

They make him lie down on the dance floor. Questions are asked trying to assess the problem. They pick though his clothing and hair looking for the source of all the blood, but the general confusion is making it difficult.

"I can't find any wounds on his scalp!" one paramedic shouts to the other.

A penlight is held up in front of Hank's bloody face and he's asked to follow the light with his eyes. He doesn't do this well because he's had five cocktails.

"I'm just a bit drunk!" Hank insists.

Suddenly a SWAT team in full riot gear bolts into the bar prepared for a mass shooting.

"ALL RIGHT, EVERYONE, THIS IS NOT A DRILL!" a cop yells through a megaphone.

The DJ finally turns the house lights up and the music down. The pirate-diva is trembling. Not only has he never seen the bar fully lit, but all the patrons have their hands on their heads and are fleeing the bar in terror. He hears a discussion over police radios about a gunman. But the words *Spun* and gun have turned it into a Laurel and Hardy sketch.

"*Spun* gunman at *Spun* with a gun, 10-4?"

It isn't until he sees his white pirate shirt soaked with bright red streaks that Hank finally gets it.

He's not covered in blood: it's his hair mousse.

He used a whole can of Clairol "Flame Red" temporary foam mousse this evening mixed with a packet of cherry flavored Kool-Aid to give the color an extra boost (a recipe he's never tried before). The exceptionally vibrant color has been sweated right off his head onto his clothes and floor. It's still running down his face and torso.

The police start screaming at the paramedics, "GET HIM OUT OF HERE! WE'VE GOT TO SECURE THE BUILDING ASAP!" Their weapons are drawn and they are canvassing the area like roaches.

"Shit! This could be another Pulse Nightclub shooting! The man at least has a concussion. Let's just get the fuck out of here and take him to the ER," the paramedic says.

Hank says nothing as he's quickly strapped to a gurney and loaded into an ambulance outside. Out the window of the aid car, he sees that the entire area around *Spun* is barricaded off with saw horses. Helicopters can be heard in the distance.

There's nothing to do when the ambulance door is closed but tell the truth. But it's not over: the mass-shooting genie is out of the bottle. Within a few minutes, Hank has officially become a "case" just shy of the FBI's attention. The scanners and media don't miss a beat. The pirate-diva is cleaned up but stripped of most of his outfit (as evidence) and interrogated for hours like something out of a film noir movie.

"Red hair mousse. Clairol. With cherry Kool-Aid," he says over and over and over. Eventually, a handsome detective-apprentice gives him a ride home.

His case is passed back and forth between the paramedics and the police department. Both are humiliated by their misjudgment. But there's not a scapegoat to be had. They just want to sweep the whole thing under the rug.

Hank, however, quickly becomes a media darling, giving interviews for local TV, radio, and print wearing a more flamboyant pirate ensemble and a better recipe for his signature bright-red hair.

The biggest honor of all is being asked to be the grand marshal of his university's gay pride parade. The Friday-night drink special at *Spun* during pride weekend will be called "The Pirate-Diva": a blend of Everclear, Red Bull, and cherry Kool-Aid.

Denito

Denito is a gay god from Amsterdam. A perfect, hairless body serves him well as an online sex performer. His website is the modern equivalent of an old-fashioned peep show; a red-light district run from his computer.

Horny men chat with Denito by typing in the text window next to his video feed:

Take off ur shirt.
U R gorgeous.
Show us ur ass.
Flex ur muscles.
I want to fuck u all night long.

His blond hair and beautiful face help him entice a legion of fans from around the world. Chat is free, but if you wanted Denito to do anything sexual you have to create an account and buy his time for a private web-cam show.

I'll do whatever u want just for u ... in private.
Tip me some more, baby I'm all urs.
Private me baby
Tip me more $ baby.
I only do that in private.
More baby more.

He's his own international brand and there's plenty of him to go around. The young Adonis makes a fortune spoon-feeding his sex appeal. His career is simply being desirable.

U R perfect Denito, marry me ....

I'm on the other side of Denito's web feed, a million miles away in Illinois. I can see him, but he can't see me. Starved for affection, I spend all my time and money on him.

Once I buy his privacy, he slowly strips for me. The skimpy shirt comes off … slowly, then his pants … slowly. If I give him a sweet tip, he looks into the camera with his clear blue eyes and blows me a passionate kiss. He talks right to me, but there is no sound: we can only type.

It's not just that I want to fuck him. When I see him, I forget that I'm old and fat and unlovable. The master-lover helps me escape my shitty life.

I reload my account with money and we chat.

Wake up my soul, Denito
Teach me to love myself, U God.
Stimulate my heart, Baby. I luv u.

Denito puts his face right up to his cam and mouths, "I love you, too, Baby."

It's unbearable that he can't touch me. I believe him like a drug. His perfect face spins my heart around and around. He brings me to a warm climax every time. Yet I'm alone.

Once my computer's put to sleep, I'm pissed off. I'm smarter and better than he is. He's just a hunk of meat.

I hate u.
I hate that I need u.

I know that Denito doesn't really love me. He's gives me the same show every time. I see the cracks. He'll get what he deserves someday.

###

The downward spiral begins.

… and another show of nothing personal. He's lost. Something's spoiling him.

… and he's pensive. Denito seems distracted. He sweats. I'm watching him fall apart right before my eyes. I bet he smells bad.

… and today my lover looks worse than yesterday. His face is puffy and I see bruises. Those six-pack abs are getting soft. A remarkable deterioration is caught on camera. My mind races without a climax.

… and now the sex worker is downright sexless. But Denito continues to peddle himself at his web cam in Amsterdam. Ghetto. For Real.

… and barely conscious. Denito's new fans are not happy.

R U asleep? wake up.
Do something.
What happened to U, dude?
Are U on drugs?
U R gross
Fat Fuck. Go back to the gym.
Get sum help.

It's an Internet lynching. The idol is smashed. He's broke. His eyes twitch so he can't type anything on his keyboard. Picking at the tiny sores on his face and chest, he is bombarded by hateful messages.

UR useless Denito.
Take a shower or something.
U R disgusting.

I tune into Denito's website more than ever. I need to watch him fall apart. I get far more gratification watching him at his worst than feeding him money at his best. Dirty, dirty man.

… and Denito's downfall goes on and on. He skipped the gym but got his first tattoo: a tiny syringe under his right eye. The tattoo doesn't heal. It blends in with the other sores on his face. It's a freak show. Old fans take pity on him.

Here is some $$ 4 u to get something to eat.
Do U have a doctor?

… and Denito slumps over. His wild, straw-like hair sticks up all over the place. He stares right into the screen, his eyes bloodshot and vacant. I'm disturbed by his performance but I can't stop watching. It's hard to tell if he's online looking for a lifeline, or still looking for indulgence.

... and today's different. Denito's naked and his skin is gray. His eyes are rolled back into his head. We're still watching, but there are no comments in his chat window.

For the first time, I feel guilty. I'm worried about my boy from Amsterdam. My sick fascination with Denito speaks volumes. I'm really looking at myself.

... and I peek in on Denito, again. He's frozen. Still. I have a knot in my belly.

... and the curiosity grips me. I check back on Denito once more. He's in the exact same position. Nothing.

Something's wrong with me. I need him back the way he was.

... and I check in again. He's a lump. I don't know what to do. My computer's parked at his site while I do chores around the house. Denito is a pot that never boils. The fire's out.

... and there's movement. Two men enter the scene and urgently attend to Denito.

One checks his pulse.

The men attempt to pick him up. His body's frozen in a sitting position. He's turned to wood.

The two men pause and look at each other. One reaches up toward the webcam.

My computer screen goes blank.

A Thousand Signatures

I'VE ALWAYS WANTED TO GET MARRIED and live a gay American dream: a queer version my parents' marriage, which is still going strong. I'm not in a relationship right now, but someday I will find him.

In honor of the increasing number of states acknowledging gay marriage, I decided to wear a traditional white wedding dress to the gay pride festival. I'm not drag queen: no wig or makeup. I'm not going to wax anything. I just want to have fun with my friends and make a political fashion statement.

Finding a wedding dress to fit a man that's practical enough to party in is a challenge. I still want something that's pretty. It takes all afternoon, but I find a gorgeous wedding dress at Goodwill: a white satin number with a huge skirt and lots of lace and glitz. I decide to pass on the veil. It won't stay on my shaved head.

The dress alone is still a bit pricey for something to wear to a dirty gay bar and a parade, but I fall in love with the dress when I try it on. Shouldn't you feel love when you're wearing a wedding dress?

Once home, the dress's train is sacrificed for ease and the hem is raised to my ankles. I butch it up a bit by spray-painting my boots and leather cuffs white. The ensemble is complete and I'm a vision.

It's dusk. I get a few funny looks on the #21 bus, but everyone quickly goes back to glaring at their devices. The gayborhood is a zoo, and my friends are scattered all over the place. I get a beer and prop myself up in the corner of my favorite bar.

Only five minutes into my evening, three young guys walk up to me: out-of-towners, I can tell.

"Take off that dress and go suck some cock!" one of them says.

Frankly, I'm not surprised to hear this.

"Oh, don't worry, sweetheart. I can suck cock in my wedding dress, thank you very much."

The leader of the pack makes a squinty face.

"Why are you ruining it for us? Stop trying to force your oppressive-frilly-boring-traditional-monogamous institution on our hot-promiscuous-anonymous gay sex!"

Oh, the gays! I've been hearing this rehearsed argument for months. Can't we all just get along? They don't know me, and I'm not interested in debating them in a bar.

I'm quite shocked when all three guys dump their drinks on the skirt of my dress. I don't know what they're drinking, but it's bright red and splatters my left thigh. The three little pigs laugh and run out of the bar.

I'm must confess I'm having a Sissy Spacek-Stephen King moment. There's a part of me that wants to flee the bar in humiliation and burn the town down. If I could, I would telepathically hurl mirror balls at them and kill them.

But I just got here.

And I'm thirsty.

I look down at my dress. If I were really getting married this evening, I would call it ruined. But goddammit, I have been bullied, beaten, and spit on my whole life. This stings a bit more because I was just bashed by my own people. Yet are they really *my people*? Nonetheless, I can't let those three asshole-pigs get me down.

Everyone clears a path as I make my way to the restroom to survey the damage. Looking in the mirror, I reflect that the placement and color of the stain is reminiscent of Jackie Kennedy pink Chanel suit on the day of her husband's assassination. I decide to wear my stained wedding dress as a badge of honor just like she did as LBJ was sworn into office.

To quote Mrs. Kennedy, "Oh, no, no. I want them to see what they have done to Jack."

Naturally, my friends rally around me, but I've already let the incident go. A cute guy comes up and asks what happened and I tell my story. Then another hottie asks me. Then another. I'm getting lots of hugs and sympathy. And free drinks.

Free drinks are fabulous, but I don't really need sympathy. What those three little pigs failed to realize is that I'm not against men having hot-promiscuous-anonymous gay sex. I feel other people's sex lives are none of my business. My wedding dress and my desire for a monogamous relationship shouldn't threaten anyone's need to be adventurous.

This is a teaching moment.

I ask the bartender for a Sharpie and spread the skirt of my dress out on a table. My friend Todd prints around the hem

"*My Wedding Is None of Your Fucking Business!*" Each of my friends autograph my dress in permanent marker. Then a cute guy comes up and asks me if he can sign my dress, too. Then another. Then another.

None of Your Fucking Business becomes the slogan of the night. By last call for alcohol, my wedding dress must have close to a thousand signatures. My dress has run out of room and I start having people sign my arms and legs.

Take that, three little pigs.

Once home, I'm exhausted, but life is good.

It's probably best that my dress lives on its padded hanger inside-out to protect the signatures.

It's a work of art.

I Febreze the Hell out of the inside of the bodice and go to bed. I've got a parade to catch tomorrow at noon.

Eric In Your Bed

THANKSGIVING, 1990.

Too tipsy to drive home, your best friend, Eric landed in bed with you.

You're a gentleman. Most gay men aren't used to gentlemen. You cuddled him to sleep with your clothes on like something out of a sweet storybook. There was no sex, not even a kiss goodbye before he left your apartment for turkey and dressing with his family in Fayetteville.

You didn't plan on falling in love with your beautiful best friend, but you fell hard for Eric that night. For years since, all you could think about after sleeping with him was getting him back in your bed once more so you could make love to him.

Eric comes to visit a couple of times every year. You're still very close. There's never been any doubt that he truly loves you. But since the Thanksgiving incident, you've taken second place while he fell *in love* over and over with Joe, then Phil, then Greg, then Steve, then Thomas. Some of those guys were just terrible. Good riddance to bad gays.

You've had boyfriends over the years, too. Good ones and bad ones. But you always find yourself drifting back to your sweet best friend and that Thanksgiving Eve cuddle. You can't seem to get out of the hole he dug in your heart.

It's Thanksgiving again, twenty-five years later. You're both single and in your forties now; fatter and wiser. Eric's driven six hours to visit you for *this* holiday: an invitation that was no accident. You make dinner together and practically force too much wine down his throat while you stick with Sprite.

Handsome as ever, Eric is right where you've wanted him for the last two decades: back in your bed. How can he resist you? You still hope that he'll someday love you the way you've always loved him.

Careful, mister: you might make a fool of yourself.

Eric is asleep. You cautiously slide in bed next to him and wrap your arms around him like it's 1990. Kissing him on the lips and waking him up would be too scary, so you resist. You want to feel *this* inside *that* but you don't dare to fuck up the friendship. You wait for the earth to move or a sign from God while you listen to him gently snore.

It's not fair. The two of you know each other better than you know yourselves. Nobody makes him laugh like you do and you're the only one who knows all his secrets. You have all the facets of a real relationship with Eric except for sex.

He belongs with you. You'd marry him in a heartbeat, but he doesn't desire you. Why do all those other guys get the honor of intimacy with this beautiful man? It makes you angry.

Another night with Eric in your bed is more than you can bear. So close yet so far. You can feel his heart beating while yours is breaking. You'll always be just "the best friend" if you don't do something about it.

Do something.

Make something happen.

Anything.

Take it and make it yours.

You let go of Eric and go to the bathroom to find a small pair of scissors. Back in your bedroom, you sit on the edge of the bed and cut a small chunk of your sleeping best friend's dark hair from the back of his head: a lovelock with a few gray hairs in the strand.

The gesture is right out of some old gothic romance novel. It's cheesy and stupid, maybe even a little creepy. You're no Delilah, but you've got to admit you feel a little bit empowered. You're entitled to the token and he'll never miss it out of that head of thick hair. You deserve something personal of his to cherish when he's not around. Maybe possessing his hair will give you some sort of aphrodisiacal appeal.

You nervously place the lock of Eric's hair in a clean white envelope and put the envelope in that dirty old Bible for safekeeping. Yes, it's strange, but a Bible seems like a good place to keep something that you value. You'll find a better place for it later.

It's dawn after the longest night of your life. Sadly, the trim is all you have the platonic nerve for this Thanksgiving. You're going to be okay. You always have been and you always will be. It just wasn't the right time for a declaration of romance. You still have your lovelock, don't you? That's better than nothing.

Eric wakes up and doesn't say a word about the hair cut from his head. You two finish off the pumpkin pie for breakfast, then he gets dressed and packs up, leaving you with all the leftovers. There's a long goodbye in the driveway, then you watch him drive away. Thanksgiving's over. Now it's Black Friday.

Back to reality. It takes a couple of hours to clean the kitchen, then you start some laundry. While changing the sheets on your bed you find a piece of paper under your pillow. It's folded in half. You open it and find a lock of freshly cut dark hair with a sprinkling of gray. It's a much longer piece of Eric's hair than what you cut. It's held together with a piece of dental floss tied in a bow. Inscribed on the note is a message in Eric's handwriting: *I love you, too. See you at Christmas.*

Remembering Dick And Jayne

EVERYONE AT THE HARRIS BARGAIN MART loves Dick. He knows all of us by our first names. He's lived in Robinson his whole life.

Dick was actually one of the very first customers I rang up at my cash register. I remember it well. Gina was training me and told me to ring him up for fifty dollars.

I was confused because Dick didn't have any merchandise to ring up. No cart or basket and nothing in his hands.

"Go ahead. Just punch in *sale* and *$50*. He comes in on the first day of every month and this is what we do for him. Don't worry, Mr. Harris knows all about it."

I was afraid to ask questions since I was new at the store. Dick was all smiles that day as he handed me two twenty-dollar bills and one ten. I tore the receipt off the register for his sale (of nothing) and handed it to him.

This has been going on for the whole two years I've worked at the store. He shops here pretty regularly and usually buys stuff for his shop like oil and antifreeze. I've seen him buy clothes here, too. He pays for all that stuff like anybody else, but once a month there's always a strange, phantom purchase for fifty dollars. It doesn't really matter, because he's one of the nicest guys you could ever meet.

None of us knew Dick had cancer, and it was a shock when he died so young. He was only forty-one years old. Mr. Harris closed the store down and the whole staff was paid to go to Dick's parents' church for a memorial. The nine of us from Harris's sat in a pew together surrounded by a small turnout of about twenty people. The preacher's eulogy was very generic. Then someone went up to the podium and started telling stories about someone named Jayne.

"Who's Jayne?" I whispered in Gina's ear. "Are we at the right memorial?"

A few more folks got up and talked about Jayne, then Mr. Harris took a turn at the podium. I was surprised to see he had put together some notes.

"Ladies and Gentleman, My name is David Harris and I own Harris Bargain Mart out on Route One in Robinson. I want to take this opportunity to talk about both Jayne and my good friend, Dick.

"Jayne" was a chubby little girl who came into the store every day after school on her bike to pick up the *Daily News* for her parents. She always wore overalls and was a shy and awkward child. It was like she was trying to be invisible. The staff watched Jayne grow up over the years, but she rarely spoke to any of us in the store until she got a little older. Jayne went away to college and we never saw her again.

"About twenty years later, a sturdy, handsome man named Dick came into my store and asked to speak to me privately.

He looked familiar, but I couldn't place him. Once I closed my office door, he introduced himself as Jayne and explained that he was living his life happily as a man now. I'll be honest: there was a whole bunch of things going on in my head at that moment. But it got even more confusing when Jayne, now Dick, handed me an envelope with a fifty-dollar bill.

"What's this for?" I asked.

"Mr. Harris," he said, "I have a confession to make.

"You see, ladies and gentlemen, my store had a very big problem with shoplifting back in the late 1980s. And our biggest losses were in the toy aisle. Someone was stealing all my Hot Wheels cars. I had barely stocked the shelves before someone would cut open the package with a pocketknife and steal them. It made me so mad at the time! I suspected a couple of the boys in the neighborhood were the thieves. I had a bunch of staff meetings and we set up a whole sting operation to catch the crooks, but we never did.

"The Hot Wheels thief was Jayne.

"Jayne was also stealing men's clothes from the store. And tools. And anything *masculine* she could get her hands on from age eight until she was eighteen. She would tuck things into her overalls or her pants and none of us in the store had any idea it was her.

"So on that day in my office, Dick was ready to make amends for his actions as Jayne. He had kept track of every item he shoplifted over the years. Dick showed me Jayne's tattered notebook, which was also stolen. It logged the price and a running total of what he owed my store. I admired the man Dick had become. He wasn't rich, but I was delighted to let him pay back the whole three thousand, three hundred seventy-two dollars and eighty-eight cents in fifty-dollar installments so he could clear his conscience."

Mr. Harris ended his eulogy by talking about what a wonderful friend Dick was. He gave him a lovely tribute, but there was very little response from the people in the room. It was clear to me that what little bit of family that was there didn't appreciate the shoplifting story. I got the feeling they didn't accept him for who he really was.

Standing outside the church, Gina asked Mr. Harris how close Dick came to paying off the total before he died.

"Close," he said. "There was one hundred twenty-two dollars and eighty-eight cents left to pay."

Without even thinking about it, Gina, myself, and the rest of the employees of Harris's Bargain Mart dug into our wallets and purses, assembled the balance in cash, and handed it to Mr. Harris.

"Go put that in the collection plate," he told us.

Peach Polyester Pantsuit

Every Monday I sit in the circle with eight strangers. It's always been hard for me to sharing my feelings with my friends and family, let alone outsiders. The room's stuffy: no windows and very bad lighting. And the chairs are deathly uncomfortable.

The demographic of my grief group is an odd mix. I've privately nicknamed each member in my head according to their fashion sense: cowboy, lawyer, journalist, hippie, housewife, dancer, and student. I'm sure everyone has tagged me the snobby, homosexual fashion designer. It's almost true: my clothes and a fancy degree from FIT label me. But I'm really shyer than a snob. If they only knew that I grew up in rural Illinois.

I'm mourning the death of my mother. The group leader has helped by offering different topics and assignment that are meant to help one cope with our loss. This is our last meeting and the group's assignment was to bring in something that belonged to our loved one.

"Who wants to do their show and tell first," the leader asks.

I don't want to go first, so I sit quietly and listen to

presentations about a wife's pillow; a son's toy; and a friend's favorite coffee mug.

My mother would get a kick out of this. She enjoyed get-togethers, but I can't say that I do. She and I loved each other like crazy but we didn't have as much in common as we used to. I still owe who I am to her. I wouldn't say that we grew apart; I'd say that she allowed me to blossom. She was always there for me and taught me to be proud of who am, especially after I came out. I wouldn't have had the guts to go into fashion if she hadn't taught me how to sew when I was a little boy.

It's my turn to share. I stand up and unzip my eight-hundred-dollar Louis Vuitton garment bag. I carefully reach in and pull out my mom's favorite outfit: a homemade peach-colored polyester double-knit pantsuit. I'm still not sure why I kept the ugly thing. Seeing the monstrosity again makes my stomach cramp a bit.

"Would you like to tell the group a little about what you brought?" the group leader asks.

It would be rude for me to say that I fucking hate this tacky, ill-made pantsuit. I pause and find better words.

"My mother wore this a lot. She bought the fabric at Walmart and made it herself several years ago."

The room's very still.

"I offered to take her clothes shopping in the city but she wouldn't go. I even offered to have my staff make her a whole wardrobe out of nice fabric from the garment district. She wasn't interested."

A woman in the group asks if she can touch it. I'm kind of weirded out by the thought that anyone would want to examine the jacket and pants. Mom was nothing more than a home sewer. She never finished the seams on anything she made and her top stitching was always crooked. I'm embarrassed by a stain that's been on the jacket for years.

"Why didn't you bury your mom in this pantsuit?" someone asks.

"There was no funeral. She was cremated."

"Do you have a picture of her in the pantsuit?"

I reach into my pocket, pull out my phone, and scroll to a picture of Mom and me taken when I took her to see her first and only Broadway play. That was a fun night. I had just moved her to the city so we could be together after she was diagnosed. You can only see the jacket and a little bit of the pants in the picture because she's sitting in her wheelchair. My phone is making its way around the circle.

"She looks very happy. I can tell in the picture that she's very proud of you."

I explain to my group how angry the pantsuit has made me for the last several months. She wasn't that sick when I first got her to New York City. My mother proudly wore that peach number to the Statue of Liberty, the Metropolitan Museum of Art, and Yankee Stadium. We always had a great time, but I wanted to shake her and tell her to put on a better outfit. It was easier to get mad at her clothes than it was to be mad at her for dying. We never talked about the fact she was going to die so soon.

I get it now. She was a seventy-three-year-old widow who'd never even been on an airplane until she got cancer. She should have worn whatever she wanted to wear. But as a fashion designer, I had trouble thinking, *It's just clothes*.

Fair is fair. I remember her begging me a few times not to wear my Prada and Gucci into the Robinson Walmart when I came home to visit.

The group says some nice things that I can't even process. I start to put the suit back into the garment bag and it hits me: I can smell my mom. I've never cleaned the pantsuit and I just got a good whiff of her that hits me hard. My mother's scent has taken over my Louis Vuitton bag.

The grief group is over. At home alone, I put the peach polyester jacket on myself, just like her, one sleeve at a time. In some crude way, wearing it is like being hugged by my mom. It's a genuine and beautiful moment like she was.

It's obvious to me that Mom's homemade peach polyester double-knit pantsuit must always live in my Louis Vuitton garment bag. That's exactly where it belongs.

Patsy Cline Airlines

An email from *Patsy Cline Airlines* is in my work inbox. It's got to be spam, but it somehow made it past my spam filter. The subject line reads: *Laissez-Faire*. That's a banking term: economics, whatever. This has to be a coworker's joke from inside the bank. I'm waiting for sort of flash animation to pop up and do something funny.

Is my computer going to explode?

Is this how they tell you you're fired?

I know I could get in so much trouble with the IT department, but I open it for a laugh.

There's a seating chart for an eight-seat plane in the email. At the top in bold, flashing letters it reads, "*We've got one seat left! Reserve it while you can!*"

John Denver, Buddy Holly, Glenn Miller, Rickie Nelson, Will Rogers, and Richie Valens all have a spot on this plane. The pilot and co-pilot are listed as John F. Kennedy Jr. and

Amelia Earhart. There's one seat not assigned in the back of the tiny plane next to Buddy.

Someone went to a lot of trouble on the graphics. The email looks pretty real. There's even a picture of the plane: a Hawker 400XP.

At the bottom of the email, it says that the plane will depart from LaGuardia Airport in two days. I am assuming there's a scheduled crash, too, considering the passenger list. I'm kind of amused.

What's the point of asking someone to reserve a seat on a fictitious, doomed airplane? It's not exactly a chain letter. What is this?

I know I should just delete the silly email, but I don't. I'm intrigued: if I could get away with it, would I really want to dispatch someone to their death in a fiery plane crash with Buddy Holly and Rickie Nelson? Does the empty seat have to go to a musician? Does the person need to be famous?

It's a pretty impressive passenger list. I can think of lots of famous people who deserve to be on that plane: Charles Manson, OJ Simpson, George W. Bush. Since it came to my work email address, I start considering people at work. There are a few people here that bug the shit out me, but I would pick Julia Trapnell, hands down. She's a stupid, manipulative bitch. She's really a waste flesh and doesn't contribute anything good to the bank, or to society for that matter. Life would be so much better if she was gone. I fucking hate her. I've often fantasized about throwing her out the window and watching her drop the eighty stories down to the plaza.

The hell with it: I'm signing her up. I forward the email to my anonymous account (that I use for porn) and put her name on the seating chart next to Buddy Holly and click on the box to send. What's the worst that can happen? She gets a computer virus for opening something she should have been smart enough to delete. Besides, who would be stupid enough to get on a plane with Patsy Cline Airlines painted on the side?

~~

I don't care about Julia Trapnell any more since she died. Yeah, I know, it's sad; the bitch was only thirty-two and she had family and all that crap. She continued to piss me off right up until the end.

It was a car accident, not a plane crash. And it's been a month since that stupid email. For a fraction of a second, I wonder if there's greater goings-on in the universe where if you wish for something really hard, you can make it happen, even if it is not ethical, even if it causes someone's death.

I don't believe in that. The email was some unexplained joke that I still don't quite understand. I never told anyone about it and I forgot about it ten minutes after I replied. Julia never mentioned anything to me about Patsy Cline Airlines. No one else at work ever said anything about it, either.

Everyone at the bank is being respectful about her death, but clearly she will not be missed. There's going to be a little, tiny memorial for her. A couple of people asked if I was going, and I said no. Why should I? I mean, come on: if I disliked her enough to wish her dead, wouldn't it be tacky of me to go to a celebration of her life?

~~

The elevator's full and it's taking forever. I've got my coffee in one hand and a pastry in the other. My watch says 8:30. I should already be at my desk. I push my way out on the 80th floor and make my way to the office.

It's a beautiful, sunny day. Fall is my favorite time of the year and the last thing on earth I want to do is sit at a desk and crunch numbers.

I've barely started up my computer and I hear the loudest explosion I've ever heard in my entire life. The whole building is shaking and swaying back and forth. Everyone's running to the north windows and they see that Tower One is engulfed in flames at around the ninety-fifth floor. I just heard someone say that a plane actually flew right into the building, a passenger jet.

It looks really bad. I'm glad it's not us.

We're told to stay at our desks.

It's going to be a long morning.

A Place For Dad

THE OFFICE IS AS SMALL AS a closet but decorated in very fashionable décor. It looks like something right out of a magazine. Trendy music is playing from the speakers built into the wall—a clever Pandora station I suspect. There's a thin young man behind an expensive desk whispering into his cell phone. He's young enough to be my son, maybe even my grandson. His GQ outfit and sharp haircut make me feel a bit out of place (I was lucky to even get a shower this morning and my clothes come from JCPenney). It takes a few minutes, but he finally offers his slim hand and introduces himself to me as Quince. The guy instantly makes me feel uncomfortable.

"Hello, Quince. I need your help finding a place for my father," My voice is kind of raspy today. My family's been through a lot the last few weeks and it's starting to take a toll.

Quince sits back down in his tufted leather chair and gets busy on his Apple computer. I'm quite relieved to not have to explain to anyone that my eighty-year-old father is gay. This non-profit agency is one of the few in the country that only serves the LGBT elder community. Dad's never been very hip, but luckily he chose to live the last thirty years in an urban setting that has many different gay nursing homes and skilled care facilities to choose from. It's Quince's job to find the one where my dad would be the most comfortable.

The young man gives me a form to fill out. I fully expect to have to answer a bunch of questions about his treatment and medication. Instead the form asks more questions about his personality: Dad's likes and dislikes. I just turned fifty-six and I'm straight. Some of the questions are over my head. I answer the best I can and hand the clipboard back, leaving many blank spaces on the paper.

Quince spends a few minutes quietly typing into his computer. He begins grilling me.

"Was your dad ever a member of the local LGBTQ BDSM leather community?"

"No. I don't think so."

"The reason I ask is we could place him immediately over at Blake's. They have a room available, but you have to be *tied* to the leather community to qualify—excuse the pun."

We both laugh (me more from nerves). My dad wears short leather boots. I wonder if that counts.

"What about drag? Does your father do drag or openly cross dress on regular basis?"

"No. Maybe at a Halloween party or gay pride many years ago," I answer with a chuckle. My father would make an ugly drag queen.

Quince is discouraged. "Well, that rules out Susy-Q's."

Back to the gay drawing board we go.

A few tense minutes pass.

"Is he into sports? Did he ever play on any of the gay leagues? Rugby? Softball?"

I explain to Quince that my father hates all organized sports. He's more into the Arts. He still has a season ticket to the opera and the symphony and a few local theaters. Quince nods his head and goes back to his computer.

I look at my watch. It seems impossible that I've been in this office less than thirty minutes.

"I know this is a very personal question, but is your dad is a top, a bottom, or versatile?"

At first I think Quince is joking. What does that have to do with anything?"

Quince explains to me in a hushed tone, "Some gay elders have very active sex lives. The facility staff may say they don't pay attention to that kind of stuff, but we all know they do. They like to see a balance of tops to bottoms."

I classify my father as *versatile* just to be safe.

"Does your dad have a beard?"

"No."

"Can he grow one?"

"Umm, why?" I ask.

"There's a spot over at Campbell House: the 'bear' nursing home."

"My father lost all his hair to chemotherapy," I say.

Now things begin to get very real. We spend a few minutes talking about my father's prognosis. I confess that he has a few more chemo and radiation treatments left, but his doctors are quite optimistic. There's no need for hospice any time soon. He just needs more care than my family can give him at home.

"Can he walk?"

The minute I tell Quince that Dad is currently in a wheelchair, he flinches. The look on his face tells me that I'm shit-out-of-luck.

"I'm so sorry. I should've asked that question sooner. This agency only serves gay men who are spryer and able to get around and still have some fun."

"Didn't this office start off in the nineties as a place to help gay men dying of AIDS?" I ask.

"Yes it did," Quince says with a smile. "But luckily with PrEP and other medical advances, we don't have to do that anymore. Gay men are living longer and happier lives and this agency has shifted its focus to that. I plan on living to be a hundred. Thirty years ago, you'd never hear someone like *me* say that."

My meeting with Quince ends with a thud.

It took two weeks, but I found a wonderful nursing home for my father on my own—one without any gay labels. Booker Gardens is a mix of men and women from all walks of life.

It's my second visit to Booker Gardens, and I hear a curious beat coming from the rec room. I look in and find my father sitting in his wheelchair with about twenty other residents facing him. They're all laughing and waving their arms in the air in unison.

My father is leading a movement class to the Village People's song "YMCA."

Dad is right where he belongs.

The Truck

SEVEN HOUSES IN A SEMICIRCLE FRAME The Grove with a circle drive and a small traffic island in the middle. It's quiet as the summer evening approaches. The temperature's cooling everything off as the sun begins to set. Yet there's always a feeling of anticipation. The residents listen, peek out of their curtains. Everyone knows where their money and shoes are.

At about 8:45 p.m., a deep base can be heard in the distance. The beat vibrates louder and louder and there's an audible electronic jingle and some faint vocal track in the air:

Ahhhhhhhh, love to love ya, baby.

"I can hear it!" Myrtle Webb yells to her husband from the living room window of 3221.

Everyone's starting to get excited. Simon Stimson from 3226 is running around like a chicken with his head cut off.

"I see it! The cocktail truck is coming! The cocktail truck is coming!" Loella Soames screams. She's already jumping up and down in her front yard waving a fistful of ten-dollar bills.

About fifty residents of The Grove are gathering in the middle of their cul-de-sac as the twenty-foot RV gets closer and closer.

"George, Rebecca, stay in the house. Call the sitter. This is Mom and Dad time," Julia Gibb reminds her little ones. Mrs. Wilder from 3230 is already preparing a big bowl of fruit punch with Benadryl to administer to all the kids door to door.

The cocktail truck's been making the rounds for about thirty years: same branding, same uniforms (now vintage). It's a mom-and-pop business that only serves two dozen neighborhoods and nobody seems to know its schedule. But from May to September, around sunset, everyone knows they can get a visit.

"Please, oh, please, oh please! I'm thirsty!" Miss Thornton says, standing out by the mailboxes.

There's always a female DJ dressed as 1980s Madonna spinning dance tunes in the back of the cocktail truck. Her dance tracks get everyone bouncing and swinging.

Colored Fresnel and LED are swaying all over the sky and streaming off the giant mirror ball on the roof. The lights quickly transform the mid-century houses of The Grove into the walls of a dazzling nightclub that would rival Studio 54.

Joe Cromwell from 3224 almost pees his pants as the cocktail truck turns into the cul-de-sac. A few stragglers are walking alongside the vehicle. God only knows where they're from. Depending on how far away the music can be heard, the truck can draw an enormous multi-neighborhood crowd of several hundred people. The klieg light pointing in the sky tells everyone where to go.

When the truck finally arrives, two bouncers that look like the '80s duo Wham (the owner's sons) jump out of the passenger door. The blond one starts setting up sawhorses to block off traffic. The dark-haired one is responsible for several feet of velvet rope and stanchions to keep the crowd in line before they begin checking IDs. One by one, the folks of The Grove step up and order their drinks from the bar station window that folds down on the passenger side of the RV.

"What'll you have, baby?" the bartender dressed like Billy Idol asks.

"I'll have a *Bee Gee* on the rocks with no lime."

"What about you, sugar?"

"*Disco Inferno*. Make it a double."

Gloria Gaynor, KC and the Sunshine Band, Cher: the music and the liquor builds a full-fledged party. People are happy and smiling and hanging all over each other. The basketball court in the driveway of 3222 has become a dance floor. Some folks sneak behind the shed at 3220 to smoke some weed. There may be a little cocaine back there, too.

"The cocktail truck has been so random this summer. I'm so glad we were picked this evening. I had a hell of day at school and I just want to relax and cut loose a little," Mr. Willard tells Sam Craig. He teaches at the university and rents out his basement to his students.

"I know. This is so much more fun than that sports bar truck," Sam says.

For four hours, the truck serves the residents of The Grove. But not surprisingly, things get a little messy.

Simon Stimson has passed out on the traffic island again and Mrs. Soames is sitting in the middle of her flower garden. She drank too fast and now she's got a headache. An altercation is happening between Wally and Emily behind the truck. She's been flirting with Joe Cromwell again. Wham takes care of the problem quickly and makes Wally go inside his house.

"Last call. Last call for alcohol," comes over the loud speaker as the DJ-Madonna plays "Never Can Say Goodbye."

Dr. Gibbs just got home from the hospital. "Fuck me! Did I miss it?" he asks his tipsy wife.

"Just in time. Here, honey, finish my *Hustle* and I'll get us two more."

"Thanks, dear. Are the kids asleep?"

"Yeah. They drank Mrs. Wilder's punch right after the drag show." Rebecca slurs her words as she orders another round and slips the Billy Idol-bartender her cell phone number.

It's time to wrap up the evening. The Wham-bouncers walk around the cul-de-sac and start collecting drinks and picking up trash out of the yards. They dutifully point people in the right direction and make sure they get safely into their own houses. Billy Idol and Madonna shut down their stations and have a smoke.

It's 2:20 a.m. and everyone in The Grove is hopefully asleep. Once again, the cocktail truck has turned upper-middle-class adults into giddy children, and nobody got a DUI.

The rig pulls out of the cul-de-sac and exits suburbia. It will be cleaned and restocked for tomorrow night's surprise visit to Loman Way.

The Vest

THEY WERE A CINCH TO MAKE, really: eight loaded pipe bombs, one detonator circuit, a broken battery pack and some copper wire all rigged to a utility vest purchased from a big box store. The tutorial from YouTube was quite helpful.

I'm dead inside. I'm so fucking hurt by my own people. I swear it used to be better when we were suppressed. Being gay was sexy and dangerous thirty years ago. My community stood up for each other back then. Now we are our own worst enemies. We've become monsters: square-headed Frankensteins with six-pack abs judging each other. Young queers failing history because it got old. No longer relevant after forty.

I don't have a twenty-nine-inch waist anymore.

My hair fell out years ago.

I'm don't have a fashionable closet or car or house or job or friends or life.

I'm worthless. Unlovable.

Their world would be better if I weren't in it, they think.

I suppose I'm just as bad as "they" are, you know… but I can't take this anymore. Something must change tonight.

Yes, I'm scared, but I have to do this.

Swish.

The vest adds forty pounds to my frame. How do I look now?

I offer my ID and pay the ten-dollar cover and no one bats an eye. "Ever see anyone wear cleats to a gay bar?" I ask the bouncer as he stamps my wrist for the last time.

I'm furious, but all I want is a hug. I just want someone to look me in the eyes and stop me or love me. Instead I'm ignored by the throngs of trendy men in their labels and tees.

A fruit loop around the club: there are distinct rooms for me to choose from. I could detonate upstairs where the leathers hang out or on the patio with the young pups. How about right in the middle of the dance floor with all the tweaked twinks? I wish I had four vests, but I only have one.

I pick the main bar by the pool tables with my least favorite bartender: the one-who-rolls-his-eyes-at-everyone-unless-he-wants-to-fuck-you. I put my goggles on and my earplugs in and order one last drink.

"Rum and Diet Coke, please."

The asshole bartender slides the drink across the bar to me. I yank the cord on my vest for all that I'm worth and I'm lifted six inches off the sticky floor. My knees buckle and my arms bounce out like wings.

I see through my mean goggles that my vest was a success. I just bombed a thick coat of glitter all over everyone and everything within a hundred feet of me. There's spitting and coughing, slipping and sliding, but no one is *really* hurt.

Asshole Bartender takes his glasses off and shakes his hair and clothes. His eye sockets are the only thing not caked in glitter.

I'm shaken, but I feel more alive than ever.

I won't be coming back to this bar ever again.

Original Publishers

"A Place for Dad" and "Eric in Your Bed" were first published by *Jonathan Magazine*.

"A Thousand Signatures" was first published by *Talking Soup*.

"Robinson, IL" was first published as "Arkansas I-40" by *The Fem*.

"The Bohemian Medusa" was first published by *The Round Up*.

"Sunday Drive" was first published by *Everyday Fiction*.

"Cornstalks" was first published by *Everyday Fiction* and later, *Great Jones Street*.

"Denito" was first published by *This Zine Will Change Your Life*.

"Eighty-Five Days" was first published by *The Rain, Party, and Disaster Society*.

"Have a Cookie" was first published by *Mad Swirl*.

"The Kiddie Pool," "Patsy Cline Airlines," and "The Truck" were first published by *The Queen Mob's Tea House*.

"The Miller Family Reunion" was first published by *Specter Magazine*.

"Mr. Blue" was first published by *Bare Back Magazine*.

"My Cousin Deborah" was first published by *Bay Laurel*.

"Peach Polyester Pantsuit" was first published by *Short Fiction Break*.

"The Pirate Diva" was first published by *Sonder Magazine*.

"Denny" was first published as "The Prince of Eighth Street" by *Fuck Fiction*.

"Remembering Dick and Jayne" was first published by *Glitterwolf Magazine*.

"The Sissy Test" was first published by *Chelsea Station* and later by *Great Jones Street*.

"The Vest" was first published by *The Rain, Party, and Disaster Society* and later by *Great Jones Street*

About the Author

Dennis Milam Bensie's poem "Eight Ball" was published in *Greater National Society of Poets, Inc.* in 1980 when he was a freshman in high school. It was featured thirty years later his memoir, *Shorn: Toys to Men*.

Short stories and poetry by Dennis have been featured in numerous publications. His essays have been seen in *The Huffington Post, Boys on the Brink*, and *The Good Men Project*.

Bensie has written two more memoirs for Coffeetown Press. *One Gay American* is a romp through America's gay history while Bensie created his own gay history. *Thirty Years a Dresser* chronicles Dennis' career working backstage in professional theater.

www.ingramcontent.com/pod-product-compliance
Lightning Source LLC
Chambersburg PA
CBHW030211130726
47898CB00012B/971

* 9 7 8 1 7 3 6 2 8 2 2 1 2 *